BEFORE

BEFORE

A NOVEL BY

BARRY GRAHAM

WITH STORIES 1987 – 1992

INCOMMUNICADO PRESS
P.O.BOX 99090 SAN DIEGO CA 92169 USA

ISBN 1-888277-04-1
First Printing

Cover photo "Monica with Candle in Mouth / Yellow"
by Richard Kern.

Book design by Gary Hustwit

Some of the short stories included in this book were first published
in the UK under the title *Get Out As Early As You Can*
(Bloomsbury).

Printed in the USA

CONTENTS

BEFORE --- 13

GET OUT AS EARLY AS YOU CAN --------------------- 101

WHAT GOES ON ------------------------------------ 133

AND I THINK TO MYSELF,
   WHAT A WONDERFUL WORLD ------------------- 149

BODILY FUNCTIONS ----------------------------- 152

HOLDING BACK THE DAWN ------------------------ 154

QUARTET:

   LET NOTHING YOU DISMAY --------------------- 159

   THAT SUMMER --------------------------------- 164

   NORTHERN LIGHT ----------------------------- 178

   TIDINGS OF COMFORT AND JOY ---------------- 182

THE MEDAL --------------------------------------- 184

QUEST FOR MAUREEN --------------------------- 186

WHAT ABOUT THE MONSTER? -------------------- 187

THE PLACE --------------------------------------- 192

WEDNESDAY NIGHT ------------------------------ 194

THE KILLER -------------------------------------- 196

EITHER/OR --------------------------------------- 198

"i am the grandchild of strife, of dreams that have struggled and died in the streets and living rooms of the twentieth century. make way for these words and remember what i say: it will take a bullet in the heart to force my silence."

– Peter Plate

This book is dedicated to Chrissie Orr, Ken Wolverton, Rowan Orr Wolverton.

ACKNOWLEDGMENTS

Except for the novel *Before,* all these stories appeared in my UK collection *Get Out As Early As You Can,* which was published in 1992. My thanks to Mike Petty for that.

The quote from Norman MacCaig is from his poem "You Went Away" which is in his *Collected Poems.* The one from Lynne Tillman is from her story "To Find Words," which is in her collection *The Madame Realism Complex.* The one from Dennis Cooper is from his novella "Safe," which is in his collection *Wrong.* The quotes from Leonard Cohen are from "Sisters of Mercy," on his album *The Songs of Leonard Cohen,* and "Take This Longing," on *New Skin for the Old Ceremony.* The quote from Alexander Trocchi is from *Cain's Book.* The ones from Steve Jinski are from his songs "Smiles and Blisters" and "Don't Go Away," on his album *Eventually.*

The epigraph to this volume is from *Black Wheel of Anger* by Peter Plate.

FOREWORD

There are people who have made my move to the US less rough than it otherwise would have been, and who have provided me with light through some dark times. Among them are: Chrissie Orr, Ken Wolverton, Scott Krause, Lynne Tillman, Bett Williams, Dennis Cooper, Anjii Solano, Hal Sirowitz, Amy Melcher, Peter Plate and Karra Bikson, Lisa Miller and Carolyn Black.

Thanks also to Gary Hustwit and Elyse Cheney.

And to Marina Blake, for unflagging belief in me and my work.

And to Alanna, for all the coffee refills and the best smile in town.

And, at the UK end, to: Jim Murray, Keith Mackie, Toni Davidson, Brent Hodgson, Janaka (Alan Spence), Irvine and Anne Welsh, Fleur Sauvage Van Der Laan, Claire Scrivener, Chantelle Duncan, Gilly Gilchrist, Gerry Loose, John Hart, Stewart Home.

This is a work of fiction.

Suddenly, in my world of you,
You created time.
I walked about in its bitter lanes
Looking for whom I'd lost, afraid to go home.

– Norman MacCaig

She is lost at sea and cast in doubt.

– Lynne Tillman

Now I'm too embarrassed to think of the people I care about
dead, and those who I love may as well be starring in their lives
around me, and I one of tons of admirers breezing by.

– Dennis Cooper

for Fleur Sauvage Van Der Laan
with everlasting love

ONE

It was the least hip music club in town. The guy who ran it was a talentless musician who wrote maudlin, introspective songs influenced—he said—by Ian Curtis and Leonard Cohen. He told his friends that he saw himself as a contemporary hybrid of the two. Venue managers didn't share his opinion—few would give him a gig, and the two or three who did were so traumatized by his performance that they told him never to come near their clubs again, even as a member of the audience.

So he'd hired the back room of an unpopular bar and organized a monthly club, with himself as the headline act. He didn't have enough money to book professional musicians, so he named the club Songwriters' Open Showcase and announced that anyone who came along and paid to get in could perform a fifteen-minute set. Consequently, the club was always filled to capacity. Every undiscovered genius within a twenty-mile radius who owned an acoustic guitar would show up, ready to share their bedroom blues. There was no actual audience; nearly everyone who came wanted to perform.

Françoise wasn't aware of this. She had only been in the country for two weeks. The night she wandered into the club was the night of the Open Songwriting Competition. This event was held about three times a year at the whim of the organizer. Françoise hadn't come along on purpose; she'd just been walking past the venue and noticed the details chalked on a blackboard outside. Inside, she stood at the bar and didn't talk to anyone. Her English was good, but she didn't have confidence in it. She ordered a beer by mumbling and pointing. As she drank it she was aware that a number of people were staring at her, but she didn't worry about it. She was used to it.

After a while the organizer came up to her and, unable to say what he meant, asked her if she wanted to enter the competition. "All right. But I don't have a guitar." He said she could use his. "Thank you." Would she like a drink? "I have one."

The club didn't have a good atmosphere. The throng was silent during each performance, but everyone was impatient for their own turn. None of the acts were impressive. Françoise felt sorry for them.

Then it was her turn. The organizer handed her a guitar. She checked that it was in tune, then walked to the microphone. For the first time, the assembly of egos became an attentive audience.

"Hello. My name's Françoise. My name is French, I'm Dutch and this song is Spanish." Some people laughed. Someone shouted *Go for it*. Françoise laughed, then played the song. She had composed the music, but the lyrics were adapted from a famous Spanish poem. Her singing voice was deep, a little like Nico's but with some range and a lot more warmth. The audience applauded when she'd finished, though the applause might not have been for the song. If this was a film, Françoise would finish her song, put the guitar down and, as an electrified audience stood up and applauded, she'd walk out of the club without waiting to find out whether she'd won the competition. All night, everyone would talk about her. And none of them would ever see her again.

As it was, she smiled, gave the guitar back to the organizer, went to the bar and got another beer.

I'm remembering this as I sit at a table in the cafe/bar of an art-house cinema. It's appropriate. Françoise's life was a life, not a film. But I'm remembering it as a film, and presenting it to you as a film. Otherwise I don't know what it means or how I can bear it.

Françoise sat in the club until it closed. She wasn't placed among the winners of the competition. The overall winner was an Englishman who'd sung a Dylanesque political song in an American accent.

A few men tried to talk to her. She was hostile towards them, not because she felt that way, but because it was the only way to get them to leave her alone. She drank two more bottles of beer, making them last as long as she was able to.

As she was leaving, the organizer asked her if she would play at the club again. She pretended that her English was worse than it was, and he gave up trying to get through to her.

Outside, the streets were crowded as people poured out of closing bars and headed home or to nightclubs. There were the usual fights over taxis. Françoise walked past it all, not looking at any of it. She slowed down when she saw a man and a woman standing under a streetlight. The woman was crying and her body was shaking. Her hands were pressed to her face and she was saying, *"Please don't hurt me."* The heavy, belligerent-looking man was talking to her soothingly, stroking her arms, trying to embrace her. Françoise couldn't tell whether he was menacing her or trying to help her. She decided not to interfere. They were drunk, and she was afraid that they both might turn on her if she said anything. She quickened her walk. Wrapped in her long coat and with the streetlights casting her shadow on the sidewalk, perhaps she imagined that she looked like Alain Delon in *Le Samourai.*

The hill was an area of wilderness in the middle of the city. Françoise didn't know its name. She was curious to know, but if she asked anyone they might wonder about her connection with it and figure out why she never said where she lived. The hill was well-known as a gay pick-up spot. She never had any idea about that, because in all the nights she spent there she never saw another person.

There were no streetlights on the hill. Françoise climbed slowly, following the path, letting her eyes adjust to the dark. It wasn't really dark, it just seemed that way at first. There was the light from the city below, and the broad illumination of the sky. Françoise could soon see everything on the hill: every tree, bush, park bench.

She went to the cluster of bushes where she'd left her ruck-sack and sleeping bag. She left them there every day, and they were always there when she returned at night. Both came from the army surplus store in Rotterdam and were dark green, so probably no one saw them among the leaves.

Françoise took off her coat and boots and got into the sleeping bag. It was slightly damp, having been rained on earlier in the day. Françoise didn't care. Her body heat would dry it. She crawled under the bushes, then rolled up her coat and rested her head on it.

On one or more of the nights Françoise spent on the hill, I was probably sitting at a table in a small Italian diner across the street from its foot. As Françoise lay in her damp sleeping bag, I drank tea, scribbled in my hardback notebook or talked with my friend Niall. At a nearby table, a group of old people sat talking in the frightened, apologetic voices some people have at that age.

The city's main railway station was near the hill. All night Françoise heard the trains. They kept waking her. In a cluster of bushes not far from hers, two men were kissing. Françoise wasn't aware of them. One of the men had been cruising the hill for years. The other had never been with a man before. He loved and was repulsed by the feel of the man's tongue in his mouth. But he got nervous when the man wanted to fuck him. It wasn't really a fear of AIDS; the man had a condom. It was just too sudden, too soon. Too overwhelming. He jerked the man off, and the man did the same for him.

A train rumbled under the hill. Françoise turned over, awake and uncomfortable. The men walked away from each other without saying anything. How do I know? I don't.

The trains became less frequent. It was almost dawn. Françoise cried a little, thinking about Tom.

Then she slept.

TWO

Tom Vince Quinn was often described in the press as "a difficult actor," a description he liked. He had come late to his vocation; he hadn't started drama school until he was twenty-six. After graduating, he quickly made up the lost time. A series of film and theater appearances brought him a reputation as one of America's most original and talented actors.

He was versatile. He could do naturalistic film and physical theater. He wasn't offered as much work as you might expect his acclaim to have brought him, because of what one theater director called "his desperate need to be alternative." Tom denied this, saying that he simply refused to consider work that didn't interest him. Trouble was, what interested him tended to be the sort of show that's more interesting to take part in than to watch.

When he appeared in a decent show, he could be astonishing. I once saw him in a play in which he played a man who went blind. At the climax, Tom blindfolded himself, then groped his way out of the theater. The audience followed. Outside was a busy main road. We watched as Tom stumbled into the traffic. There was nearly a pile-up as cars braked or swerved. Somehow, none of them hit Tom. He did that for five consecutive nights and didn't get run over. When the police complained after reading about it in the tabloids, he ignored them. The tabloids said he was "dangerous and irresponsible." The hip magazines said he "showed a commitment to art of an intensity that is almost unprecedented." Off the record, both sides agreed that he was mental. But it made for great theater.

He wasn't a pretty boy. At thirty-seven, he was almost completely bald. He had a gaunt face with big eyes and a small mouth that made him look like a pixie when he smiled and like a serial killer when he didn't.

I first met him when he was considering performing in a

play I'd written. I'd been commissioned to write it by a company who planned to premiere it at a physical theater festival in New York. The venue was booked, the posters printed. Then the actor who was to play the lead—and for whom I'd written the part—said he was pulling out. He was tired of the company's vapid and arrogant director. And now he'd been offered some well-paid TV work, the dates of which clashed with the dates of my play. I told him I didn't blame him; if I'd known in advance what a prick the director was, I wouldn't have gotten involved in the first place.

Paul, the director, phoned me a day or so later. "We might have found a replacement for José," he told me. "Tom Vince Quinn's thinking about doing it."

"You're kidding. How'd you get him?" *That is, why would he want to work with a bozo like you?*

"I just called him up and asked him. He says he's interested in the project."

That weekend I was to give a reading of some of my stuff at a rave club. I didn't expect it to work—a crowd out of their tits on disco biscuits being asked to take a break from dancing to hard techno to listen to me for twenty minutes. But the money was good and the organizer persuasive. I said I'd do it.

I was sitting in the dressing room, waiting to be called, when a guy I recognized but had never met came in. "Barry?" he asked me, smiling.

"Yeah."

He held out a hand. "I'm Tom. I'm thinking about doing your play."

"Oh, hi." I shook his hand. "Yeah, it'd be great if you could do it."

"I'd like to. Paul showed me the script. It's good."

"Is Paul here tonight?"

"Nah." Tom laughed. "I was with him earlier tonight, but he wouldn't pay to get in here."

"Typical."

"You don't like him?"

"No. In fact, I'd better warn you so you know what you're getting into: Paul's a fucking waste of space. That's why José quit."

He laughed again. "It goes with the territory."

"How d'you mean?"

"All theater directors are scumbags. You need directors for film, but not for theater. A theater director is someone with an ego desperate to be in theater, but who can't act or write. So they make a career out of getting in the way of people who can."

"So they're all as bad as Paul?"

"Oh, no. Paul's the theater director's theater director. He's a lot of asshole for the one guy."

I liked Tom already. That wasn't a surprise. His personal warmth was well-known. Someone once observed that you couldn't leave him for five minutes in a room full of people without him making a new friend. Of which more later.

Before we could talk any more, I got my call to go on stage. I did and it was even worse than I'd anticipated. An audience loved-up on ecstasy would have been bad enough. But this wasn't even a proper rave; I only had to take one look at the audience to realize that they'd ingested too much coke and not enough ecky. The vibe was nasty, the kind of scene where you expect a fight to start anytime.

I read and was barely tolerated. I was lucky and only had one heckler. He kept shouting, *"Put the techno back on!"*—a line of such lacerating wit that I could think of no rejoinder. He stopped after a couple of minutes, and no one else tried to give me a hard time. Instead, most of them just talked amongst themselves, which I hated more than being heckled. At the end of my set I was pleased to go and they were pleased to see me go.

I looked around for Tom, but I didn't see him. A couple of cokeheads approached me to tell me what an awful performer I was. The manager of the club gave me my fee. I left and went home.

Paul phoned me the next day. "Why did you leave last night? I was looking for you."

"You weren't even there," I said.

"Yes, I was. I arrived just as you finished. They let me in for free because it was so late and I said I was a friend of yours."

"Mm. Did you see Tom?"

"No, he'd left too. Apparently he was in some sort of fight."

I didn't know it then, but the fight had been with the man who'd heckled me, and it wasn't so much a fight as a one-sided beating. The man's heckling had stopped because Tom had asked him to come outside and talk with him. Out in the street, Tom grabbed the man's throat with his left hand and shoved him up against a wall. He held him there and used his right hand to punch the man in the face, over and over. The man started crying, saying he was sorry, please stop, but Tom kept it going. The man didn't bleed much but his face swelled up until he could have passed for the Elephant Man. Afraid that the police might be called, Tom let go of him and walked away. Tom never knew it, but the man went blind in one eye.

Paul called me again, about an hour after his first call. "I've just heard from Tom," he said. "He's really hungover. He got wasted with Claire Scrivener after he left the club. He says you know her."

I laughed. Claire was a friend of mine. She fronted an all-female punk band, and had a capacity for alcohol and drugs that didn't seem to harm her gothic good looks and perfect figure. Tom knew her from his own punk days when he'd played in a couple of bands. On his way home from the club, he'd passed by a bar that was a popular punk hangout at the weekends. A poster listed the three bands who were on that night. Claire's was one of them. Tom went in. It was so late that the bands had finished playing, but the place was still busy. Claire was hanging out. Tom went over and talked with her. He didn't mention what had happened earlier. When the bar closed, they found one that stayed open later. Claire told him that she'd just demo'd some new songs. Tom said he'd like to hear the tape. They went to her place and listened to it. "It's good," Tom said. "Especially the screams." They were sitting on the couch in her living room. Tom was sprawled on it. Claire was curled up at one end, facing him. "I've been kidding myself that my reason for coming back here was to hear your demo," Tom said. He moved along the couch until he was next to Claire, put an arm around her, kissed her. She just sat there, didn't open her mouth, and when he tried to get his tongue between her lips she pulled away. "It's not on, Tom." He smiled and shrugged, a mixture of frustration and embarrassment. "Sorry," Claire said. She got out a bong and they got stoned. Tom tried to talk her into fucking him, but it didn't happen. He passed out on the couch just before dawn. Claire covered him with a blanket and went to bed. She was still asleep when he woke at noon and used her phone to ring Paul.

"He says he'll definitely do the show," Paul told me. "He seems to like you."

At that moment, Françoise may have been in a cafe in Rotterdam. She was with her friend Ingvild, who was supposed to be buying her lunch. After they'd eaten, Ingvild discovered that her money and bank cards weren't in the bag she'd brought out with her. Françoise didn't have enough money to pay, and she didn't have any bank cards. They ordered another pot of coffee and drank it while they tried to decide what to do. Making a run for it wasn't an option. Françoise was dressed for it in shorts and sneakers, but Ingvild wore pumps. Besides, Ingvild was quite overweight, and they both had bags that might slow them down. Françoise wasn't that worried, but Ingvild, who had probably never so much as crossed the street when the signal was red, was ready to cry.

Françoise had a harmonica in her bag. She got it out. She caught the eye of the woman working behind the counter, and smiled at her. The woman smiled back. Françoise got up and walked over to the counter. She explained the situation. The woman's smile disappeared when she realized what she was being told. "So," Françoise concluded, "I can give you my address and a promise to come back with the money, or else—" She held up the harmonica. "I can play you a song on this."

The woman looked at her for a second. Then her smile came back. "All right. But only if you play it for everybody in the cafe."

The place was busy. Françoise stood on a chair, shouted and clapped her hands for attention. She got it. "Okay, I've had lunch here and can't pay for it. So I've been ordered to play my harmonica for you. Is that okay?"

A few people clapped and whistled. She made the hipper ones laugh by playing a note-perfect rendition of Joy Division's "Love Will Tear Us Apart." Then she managed to find her way through Abba's "Money, Money, Money." That one got a grin from the woman at the counter. When Françoise had finished, the woman gave her a pot of coffee.

Françoise probably wasn't surprised. She expected people to react to her that way. One time she met me in a bar. We were going to hear Claire's band play in a club nearby. Françoise was late and arrived at the bar just minutes before we'd have to leave for the gig. She ordered a beer and I told her she wouldn't have time to drink it. "I'll take it with me, then."

"I wouldn't try sneaking it out of here," I told her. "The bouncers on the door are pretty nasty. They don't take any prisoners."

"It's all right." She smiled. "They like me already." I have that moment in my head like a snapshot in my photograph album. I had shaved her head a few days earlier and she looked incredible.

As it turned out, Tom couldn't do my show. There was a local election coming up, and Tom agreed to stand as a candidate for the Communist Party. He'd been a member for years—he was something of an unreconstructed Stalinist—and was still into it. Although there was no possibility of pulling more than a few votes, since even his friends wouldn't vote for him, he insisted that it was an important point of principle to stand. He'd be so busy campaigning that he'd have no time for rehearsals. The show was on the verge of being called off when José got in touch to say that his TV work had fallen through and so he was available again. The day before the show opened in New York, I got a card from Tom, wishing me well.

I don't know where this story is going. Not the real story. I know the narrative, the details of what happened. But I don't know what the point is. I don't know the meaning, or if there is one. That's what I'm trying to find.

The last time I saw Françoise, I signed one of my books for her. *"For Françoise—distance is no separation if we think of each other—all my love, Barry."* I don't know if it helped her, but that's something I always clung to. Whenever I got to feeling really bad, missing her so much, I'd think of her with love, think about how much I loved her, and it'd be all right. I'd imagine her wherever she was, whatever she was doing, and I'd feel better. But I can't do that now. And I don't know how to deal with it.

I'm nine years older than Françoise. So, when I was eight years old, she didn't exist. And that's how it is now. I can remember being eight, but of course I can't make sense of it that way.

THREE

At nineteen, Françoise had only been out of school for about a year. She had never been to the Rotterdam Film Festival before. Her girlfriend, Lotte, was fifty and had been going for years.

They went to see a double-bill of short American films, each one lasting about forty minutes. The first one was in grainy black and white. This had obviously not been done for arty effect, but because of a lack of budget. The film wasn't great, but Françoise was captivated by one of the actors. There was nothing conspicuous about the way he looked or talked. He was bald and nondescript, and the character he played was an inarticulate thug, so his lines were less than compelling. But he hypnotized Françoise. She stopped following the plot and just watched him. When the credits rolled at the end, she saw that his name was Tom Vince Quinn.

The second film was better. When it finished there was a panel discussion, involving the directors and some of the actors from both films. When Tom got on stage Françoise felt herself get wet between her legs. That had never happened to her before just from looking at someone.

She didn't understand much of what he said during the discussion. His accent was strong and he seemed quite drunk. He referred a lot to American politics, which Françoise didn't know much about.

When the discussion ended, she went to the cinema bar with Lotte. She was hoping that Tom would be there. He came in about ten minutes later, with the director of his film. Françoise told Lotte that she wanted to go and talk to him. Lotte realized what was going on and said she wanted to leave. Françoise asked why. Lotte said she was tired. Françoise said that she wasn't, and that she was too excited to go home so early. Lotte said that she felt tired and ill, and that it was unfair of Françoise to let her go home alone. Françoise offered to take her home, then come back to the cinema. Lotte became angry and left.

Tom hadn't enjoyed the discussion following the screening of his film. He was sure that the audience didn't understand much of what he said, and that they were indifferent to his politics. He was too drunk to be able to explain this to the audience, but not quite drunk enough to be past caring about it. Still, that was easily remedied—another couple of drinks ought to do it.

He stood for a while exchanging pleasantries with the makers of the other film. Then, with his director in tow, he headed for the bar. Mark, the director, ordered the drinks. Tom gazed around the bar.

He saw two women, probably mother and daughter, sitting at a table. The older one was ordinary looking—plump, curly brown hair going gray, a pale, lined face. But the younger woman was so beautiful that it was almost freakish. Tom had never seen a woman so beautiful, not in person, or movies, or photos, or paintings. People in the bar were openly staring at her, and it wasn't just a sexual thing—as many women as men were doing it. What made her so beautiful was beyond language; even as Tom looked at her he didn't know what it was. Part of it might have been in her tall, perfect body, but most of it seemed to be in her face. Her cheekbones and her huge smile gave her an expression both of kindness and of barely-suppressed hilarity.

The older woman left, and the younger one stood up. Tom assumed that she was leaving as well. Instead she walked towards him. He was suddenly aware that he'd been staring at her as openly as anybody else. He expected her to tell him to find something else to look at, but she smiled at him with her whole face. "I liked your film," she said in English.

"Thanks. I was really into doing it. It was such a great script, and Mark's a friend of mine. I didn't get paid much for doing it, but I really wanted to anyway. Like I was saying in the discussion, it has to be about more than that..."

Françoise couldn't understand what he was saying. "Would you like a drink?" she asked him.

"Mark's just getting me one. Do you want one?"

"You'll have to talk more slowly. I find it hard to understand."

Tom said it again, and she asked for a beer.

She sat at a table with Tom and Mark. Mark talked a lot about films, trying hard to impress her. Tom would probably have liked to, but he was too drunk and too tired. His speech slurred, and Françoise understood even less of what he said.

"How much longer are you staying in Rotterdam?" she asked him.

"Just tonight. We go back to the States tomorrow."

"Yeah," said Mark. "We've got an early flight. Eight in the morning." He looked pointedly at Tom. "You'd better turn in soon. Sleep off that booze."

Françoise noticed that he said *you*, not *we*. He didn't seem in too much of a hurry to get to bed himself.

"I'll be okay," said Tom. Mark's disappointment was palpable, but he bore it with good grace. When they'd talked for a while and he was certain that Françoise wasn't into him, he said he had to get some sleep.

"Remember that flight," he warned Tom as he stood up.

"I'll be there."

Mark shook hands with Françoise. "Nice meeting you," he said.

"And you too. I hope you have a nice journey back to America."

Mark left.

Tom was very drunk. He was near to falling asleep. Françoise put her hand on his arm and squeezed it. "Do you want to go for a walk?" she said. The proposition couldn't have been less appealing to Tom, but he nodded and heaved himself to his feet.

Outside the cinema, she pushed him against a wall and kissed him. He swayed, alternately leaning against the wall and against Françoise. He wished he weren't so drunk. He returned Françoise's kiss as best he could, taking her bottom lip between both of his and tugging at it. He wondered whether he was getting hard. Short of touching himself, he couldn't tell.

Françoise hailed a taxi. Tom fell asleep on the way to her apartment, and she had to shake him awake when they got there. She helped him up the stairs. They went straight to her bedroom and she helped him strip to his underpants as he sat on the edge of the bed. She liked his body. Although she was attracted to heavy women, she liked skinny men.

Tom got under the duvet and settled on his back, his eyes closed. Françoise took off her clothes and got in the bed with him. She pressed against him. "Do you want to make love to me?" she asked him. He didn't answer. She pulled his underpants as far as his knees, then felt for his cock. It was soft. "I can't," Tom mumbled. She stroked his cock. It stiffened a little, then no more. She kissed his neck, using her tongue. Nothing happened. "Sorry," he said. "I'm just too tired and I've had too much to drink. Maybe in the morning."

He fell asleep in a few minutes. It took her longer. She didn't turn the light off, but lay holding him, looking at his face.

When she woke in the morning she felt exhausted. She could hardly keep her eyes open. She and Tom talked for a while, but it would serve no useful purpose for me to make up what they said. Then Tom got up. Françoise looked at the clock by the bed. Six-twenty. She fell asleep. When she woke again it was afternoon and Tom was gone. She wondered if he was in America now, or still on the plane. She had never been to America and wasn't sure how long it took, but she thought he'd still be in the air.

She got out of bed. He'd left three postcards on her mantelpiece. They were identical, featuring a still from the film she'd seen him in. He'd written a message on each one. What he'd written isn't important.

☆   ☆   ☆

At that time I was living in a small room on the third floor of a large, decrepit house. It was a gray, vicious winter. I had no job. I'd wake in the mid-morning and the room would be so cold I'd be able to see my breath. I'd get up, switch the electric heater on and get back in bed until the room warmed up, which would take about an hour. During that time I'd jerk off, then read a book or magazine. Richard Brautigan's *In Watermelon Sugar* is one of the books I recall, *Your Flesh* one of the magazines. Then I'd get up again and boil my cheap electric kettle, make some tea. I'd drink it, looking out of the dirty window. Often as not, rain would be streaming down the outside of the glass, visible through the condensation on the inside. Outside, the street was empty with its broken fences and uncared-for gardens, just the odd cat or dog wandering by, going from nowhere to nowhere else. It should be filmed in sepia tones, with steel blues music as mournful accompaniment. There was something about it all that wouldn't let me sit in my room, that made me so physically restless I had to get out. I'd wrap up in a big secondhand coat and go out into the rain. The cold would numb my face, but I'd spend a few hours just walking around. I'd only go back to my room when I'd run out of places to go. If I had some money I'd go into a cafe, linger over a pot of tea and a roll. When I got back to my room I might be able to settle to read or listen to music.

Tom called Françoise from the US a couple of days later. Then he sent her a letter.

Dearest Françoise,

I'm in New York to do a show. Today I took a walk by the Hudson River. It was cold and drizzling a little, but I didn't mind because I was thinking of you. I stood and looked at the expanse of the river, and thought about boats arriving, sailing up the river from the sea. But the only boat I'd care about would be one that was bringing you to me. I wish so much that you could be here, especially since Lorne, my son, will be with me for a couple of days, and it would be wonderful if you could meet him.

Regards your coming to America—would you really think about doing it? I could send you some money every week, and you could save as well, until you've got enough for the flight. I really want you here.

Take care, my love. I read in the paper this morning that today is International Women's Day. I smiled to myself, because you are my international woman.

> *All my love,*
> *Tom*

Françoise's note of reply was pithy:

Dear Tom,
I would like to come.

> *Love,*
> *Françoise*

She sent it to his home address, not knowing where he was staying in New York. She heard nothing from him for three weeks, but she wasn't worried. She just assumed he was still in New York. Then she got a letter from him. He said he was back home and about to play Vladimir in a production of *Waiting For Godot*. He said it was a pretty straight theater company and he didn't really want to do it, but he was short of money and they were paying him well. He didn't say anything about the practicalities of Françoise's getting to the US. In fact he didn't refer to it until the end of the letter, signing off with *I wish you could be here.*

Françoise gave notice on her apartment, and began selling her possessions. She didn't have much—TV, stereo, some records and books. She didn't own her furniture—it came with the apartment. She had just about enough in the bank to buy a ticket to the US, but it would mean arriving there without money. She would have to buy a return ticket, even though she had no plan to come back. If she only had a one-way ticket they wouldn't let her in. She went to a travel agent and booked the cheapest flight they had, which wasn't cheap at all.

She'd barely seen Lotte since the night she'd met Tom.

Lotte had called her often, but Françoise hadn't called her back. She didn't want to be a bitch, she just didn't know what to say. Their relationship hadn't been good for a while. Lotte had a real problem with the age difference. They'd been together for more than a year, all during which Lotte had kept saying that it couldn't work, that Françoise was too young for her. Françoise said it was only that way if Lotte made it so. They tried living together, but that didn't last long. Lotte treated Françoise like a wayward daughter rather than a lover, complaining about her untidiness, the hours she kept, the music she listened to. Françoise moved out after a few months.

The night before she left Holland, Françoise went to Lotte's apartment. It was about nine o'clock. Lotte had been drinking. She asked what was going on, and Françoise told her. Lotte cried. She said that Françoise was behaving like a child. Françoise said, "Maybe. You keep telling me I'm almost a child." Lotte cried harder. Françoise cried too, not because she didn't want to leave Lotte, but out of sadness for Lotte hurting so much.

She kissed Lotte, licking the tears away. Then she traced the lines on Lotte's face with her tongue. Lotte became so excited that it got to Françoise too. They stood in the living room and kissed, sucking and swallowing each other's spit. Then they went to bed. Lotte came before she'd taken her clothes off, when Françoise rubbed her through her trousers. When they were naked and in bed, Lotte went down and licked Françoise, sucking on her. Wetness seeped from Lotte's mouth and Françoise's cunt until Françoise was wet from cunt to asshole. Lotte slipped a finger into Françoise's ass, knowing how much she liked that, and Françoise came, not hard, but gently and luxuriously.

Lotte wanted Françoise to stay the night, but she wouldn't. Françoise thought of movies, usually thrillers, in which the hero gets out of bed during the night, dresses and slips out, leaving a beautiful woman asleep and unaware. Françoise wished she could leave like that, but her film was a realistic one. As she walked back to her apartment she thought that getting out of the relationship had been as awkward and messy as Lotte's pulling her finger out of Françoise's ass.

She wasn't leaving much behind as the plane took off. She didn't have many close friends. Her friends from school had all gone to university and she hadn't. So she didn't see much of them anymore. She wasn't close to her parents, especially after how they'd reacted to her sexuality and her decision not to go to university. She had no job or career. She'd been surviving by freelancing as a model, sometimes for artists or photographers, sometimes for the art college.

She'd flown a lot and was used to it, but she always had a rush of excitement when the plane went so fast that it started to rise off the runway. That was why she'd booked a seat by a window, even though an aisle seat would have given her more legroom, something that mattered to someone as tall as her on such a long flight. She didn't find the sight of cloud banks very inspiring, but she wasn't prepared to miss the view during takeoff.

The flight lasted twelve hours, including an hour's stopover in an American city that wasn't where she wanted to be. She didn't eat the airline food. She was vegetarian, and the vegetables they served were dry enough to make eating them a chore. The in-flight movie didn't interest her. Instead of watching it she read Roche's *Jules et Jim*. She'd seen the Truffaut film many times without knowing that it was based on a book. The time passed quite easily, though every so often she got so cramped and fed-up sitting in her seat that she had to go to the toilet and pull faces at herself in the mirror for relief.

"And you won't make me jealous if I hear that they've sweetened your night./We weren't lovers like that, and besides it would still be all right." Leonard Cohen wrote that. I used to wonder what he meant by it, and think maybe it was something like what happened with Françoise and me. The song is on his first album. Another song from that album was used on the soundtrack of

the film *McCabe and Mrs Miller*. Nearly thirty years after writing those songs he became a Zen monk.

Françoise got off the plane. It was early evening, and it was chilly. She was nervous about getting through immigration; someone had told her that they wouldn't let you into the US unless you could prove you had plenty of money. So she'd brought a bank book that said she had some. She'd taken all her money out of the account by using automatic cash dispensers over the period of a week, taking out the maximum allowed each day. Since she never made an over-the-counter withdrawal, the figure in the book remained the same. Most of the money she withdrew had been spent on her plane ticket, and she had a little less than eighty dollars in her pocket.

She didn't need to show the book. They let her through without any fuss. She'd had to fill out a form on the plane, stating her reason for visiting the US and giving the address she'd be staying at. She'd said she was taking a holiday, and given Tom's address. She handed over the form at immigration, and the guy wished her a pleasant stay.

She walked around the airport, looking at the shops and fast-food places, listening to the accents of the people around her. It was like the American films she'd seen, and yet not like them at all. Some of these people had dental problems, and all of them had to use the toilet.

Françoise went into one of the fast-food places and bought some fries and a large Diet Coke. The fries had some kind of seasoning on them. She didn't sit down, but ate as she walked. When she'd eaten the fries and drunk the Coke, she tossed the empty cartons into a trash bin, then went outside.

It was dark now, and the cold seemed colder after the warmth of the airport. There was a line of taxis near the door. Françoise got into one of them, giving the driver Tom's address. She looked out of the window as the cab rolled along the freeway. The driver didn't chat and she was glad. She didn't feel like talking. She just wanted to see Tom. As they left the freeway, the driver asked where exactly the place was. She told him that she didn't know. She knew that he'd now feel safe to overcharge her, but there was nothing else she could have said. They drove around for a while, the driver looking—or pretending to look—for the right street. Françoise told him that he shouldn't be driving a cab if he didn't know the city. He said nothing, but they stopped outside Tom's house a minute or two later.

The fare was twenty-nine dollars. Françoise paid it resentfully, and didn't give him a tip. She got out, dragging her rucksack and holdall with her. The driver didn't help her, and when she'd closed the door he drove away without acknowledging her.

It was a quiet street, run down and shoddy. The house brought to mind the Bates Motel in *Psycho*. She rang the doorbell. It didn't work. She knocked. No answer. She knocked harder, then pounded. Still no answer. She stood back and looked at the house. No light from any of the windows. It occurred to her that Tom was probably at the theater, performing in *Waiting For Godot*.

She decided to wait until he came home. She sat on the ground by the door. She was exhausted and felt slightly tearful. After a while it started to rain, and she knew she couldn't bear to just sit there and get wet.

She picked up her bags and walked. The streets were deserted. A part of her wondered what she was doing walking along a rainy street in a city in a country where nobody even knew she was there. Then she saw a young woman coming out of a house. Françoise approached her. "Excuse me. Do you know where the Lyceum theater is?"

"Oh, yeah. Do you have a car?"

"No."

"Well, you've got quite a trek with those bags."

"That's all right," Françoise said. The woman gave her directions and told her to be careful.

The sight of the theater from the outside was enough to tell her why Tom had been reluctant to work there. Its gothic facade and steeple marked it as the theater of the Establishment, a place where classic plays would be performed with the proper reverence. Incongruously, there was a man sitting on a wooden crate outside the theater. He was selling *Grapevine*, a newspaper sold by homeless people. Not knowing, but guessing what it was, Françoise bought one from him.

He was in his late thirties or early forties. His forehead, nose and cheeks were crusted with scabs and dried blood.

"What happened to your face?" Françoise asked him.

"Somebody hit me with a rock yesterday."

"Why? What happened?"

"I was sitting here, and these guys walked up to me. One of them just smashed this rock in my face and then they walked away."

"But why would he do that to you?"

He shrugged. "I don't know. There's some crazy people out there."

Françoise stood and looked at him, not knowing what to say. She took out a pack of the sugar-free gum she chewed. "Want some gum?"

"Yeah!" The guy smiled at her. "I love gum."

"Take care of yourself," she told him as she walked away. He winked at her.

She went into the theater and found its bar. She got a beer and sat down. She didn't want to look for Tom just yet. What had happened to the guy outside had gotten to her. What the fuck was he doing to anybody, sitting there on his crate trying to sell enough papers to get a hot meal? She thought she could kill the sort of person who'd do that to him, and she'd sleep with a clear conscience afterwards. Anyone could be an asshole, but some people were just a waste of oxygen. She wanted to take the guy somewhere and buy him dinner, but she didn't have the money.

She went to the toilet, locked the door and cried. A few minutes later she felt as though she'd unloaded all the garbage she'd been accumulating all day. She wiped her face with toilet paper, then looked in the mirror. Her lips were a little puffy, but otherwise she looked all right. Men would probably find the look of her lips sexy. She smiled at the thought, then winked at her reflection.

She left the toilet, went outside and found the stage door. "I'm looking for Tom Vince Quinn," she told the man who answered her knock.

"He's onstage right now." He looked at his watch. "Should be finished in about twenty minutes."

"I'll come back then."

"Can I give him a message?" He was looking at her.

"Not really. I've just come to stay with him. He wasn't at his house, so I thought he must be here."

"Wait a minute. Is your name Françoise?"

"Yes."

"You came here from Holland?"

"Yes."

"He never said you were coming."

"He didn't know. I came to surprise him."

"Jesus." He opened the door wide and ushered her in. "That's unbelievable. God, he'll freak. He never stops talking about you."

He took one of her bags and they climbed the stairs to the actors' dressing room. "You can wait in here. D'you want coffee or something?"

"Coffee, yes, please."

He left and came back with a mug of instant.

"Thank you."

"Uh-huh. I'll have to leave you on your own for a while. I have to go downstairs and look after the door. But I'll be back. I'm not going to miss this."

☆ ☆ ☆

The perfect scene for the perfect ending of a date movie: Tom and the other actors walk along the corridor to the dressing room. They're laughing. Tom is dressed as a tramp. A bashed bowler hat is cocked on his head. He opens the door, walks into the room. Françoise is sprawled in a chair, grinning at him. Tom looks at her. Close-up of his face. Françoise stands up. He goes to her. She throws her arms around him and they kiss fiercely. She takes the hat off his head and puts it on her own, as the other actors and the stage door guy stand looking on. Freeze frame. Roll credits.

But that wasn't the end.

An hour later, she sat in the theater bar with Tom and the rest of the cast. She'd have liked to be alone with him, but it hadn't happened that way. Tom had insisted that they had to hang out with his colleagues. They sat and listened to Tom talk about the play. "It's wearing me out," he said. "I'm starting to wish Godot would actually show up, just for some variety." Different people came in and out of the bar. They all stared at Françoise. Tom enjoyed introducing her as his girlfriend. The director of the play, Benny England, came and sat with them for a while. Tom seemed to like him, but Françoise didn't. He was an awesomely fat man with the common theatrical habit of asking stupid questions in an intense, interrogative voice.

"Tell me something," he said to Tom. "How do you perform a play?"

"What d'you mean?"

"What I say. When you're acting in a play, how do you do it? What's your *modus operandi*?"

Tom looked bemused. "Well, I could probably tell you some of it, the bits that I actually know. But it'd take all night."

England shook his head, his expression one of belligerent impatience. "Nonsense. It's a simple, straightforward question that needs a simple, straightforward answer. How do you play a part? The answer is simple."

Françoise expected Tom to tell the fat man he was full of shit, but he didn't. Instead he laughed and said, "Well, maybe I'm a simpleton then, Benny. I really don't know how it's done."

"Of course you do," England clucked.

Françoise couldn't listen to any more. "How can you say something like that?" she asked him.

England took a few seconds to focus his gaze on her, as though he was doing her a favor by looking at her. Seeing how young she was, he smiled indulgently. "I beg your pardon?"

"I said, how can you say something like that to Tom? He's a very good actor."

"So I'm told."

"Well, what you're told is right. How can you tell him he knows how he does it when he says he doesn't? Are you saying that he's too stupid to realize that he knows, or that he does realize and he's a liar?"

Tom looked embarrassed. "Take it easy, Françoise. Benny's not telling me anything. We were just talking."

"*He* was talking."

England beamed at her. "And who might you be, you connoisseur of fine acting?"

Before she could answer, Tom said, "This is Françoise, my girlfriend. She just arrived today from Holland."

"Oh." England held out his hand and she reluctantly shook it. "I didn't know Tom had a girlfriend. You're quite beautiful."

Françoise nodded. "I know."

When the bar closed, Tom suggested going to a club. A couple of actors were into it, but Françoise said, "Tom, I can't. I'm so tired. I've been traveling for a day, and I carried these bags all the way from your house to here."

"A tab of ecstasy'll wake you up."

"I don't want to wake up. I want to go to bed." She was hurt that he wasn't in any hurry to be alone with her. Her arrival didn't seem to be causing much disruption to his usual routine.

"Okay," he said. He put an arm around her and kissed the side of her head. "We'd better get you home, then." He picked up her bags. "See you guys tomorrow," he told the actors.

"Nice to meet you," Françoise said. "Or most of you," she added, looking at England.

When the two of them had left, everyone talked about Françoise, and wondered how Tom, or anyone, could have gotten her.

"You could've taken it easy on Benny," Tom said as he drove.

"Why did you let that fat fuck speak to you like that?"

"He didn't mean any harm. It's just his way. He really likes me. And he's a good director."

"So what?"

"There aren't many of them around, that's what. And he's into what I do. He's given me a lot of work."

"You shouldn't let him treat you like a child."

"He wasn't really. You just don't understand what these people are like."

"He can only be like that if you let him."

Tom grinned. "Ah, the ideals of youth."

She grinned back. "Now you sound like him."

"Yeah. Next time he tells me about being an actor, maybe I should tell him about being a fat bastard."

They both laughed.

"I can't believe you're here," Tom said when he'd stopped the car outside his house.

She looked at him in the rainy dark. "I'm here."

"And I can't believe you came all this way just for me."

"I didn't come to visit Disneyland."

They got out of the car. Tom unlocked the front door of his house. "How're you going to get them to let you stay in the country?"

"I don't know."

"I could marry you."

"You could."

They went inside. The house was old, with a cold musty air. It was the kind of house that people rent rooms in, not the kind you expect a person to own and make a home in. The furniture was faded, and none of it matched. It had come from the various thrift shops that Tom had made his hunting ground since he'd managed to convince his bank to give him a mortgage.

Françoise liked the house. Tom asked if she wanted anything to eat or drink, and she said she just wanted to go to bed. Tom told her to go ahead, he'd just drink some tea and then join her.

She got undressed and got under the sheets. The bedside lamp was on. She lay and looked at the theater posters on the walls, some with Tom's face on them. She closed her eyes and thought about where she was, trying to take it all in.

She switched the lamp off and tried to sleep, but her brain was more alert than it had ever been. After a while Tom came in. She didn't say anything and he thought she was asleep. He undressed in the dark and got into bed. Françoise put her arms around him and kissed him. "I really love you, Tom."

"I love you."

She touched his cock. It was hard. But he was tense. Although he returned her deep kisses, he didn't run his hands over her as she was doing to him. When she made to straddle him and sit on his cock, he pulled her down and made her lie beside him.

"What's wrong? You don't want to make love to me?"

"It's not that. It's just that I haven't felt this close to anybody since I got divorced. That's four years. I'm a little scared."

"You don't have to be scared."

"I know. But you're going at a hundred miles an hour and I'm going at thirty. Tonight, can we just lie here and hold each other?"

"Anything you want." She kissed him, and they lay naked in each other's arms until they both fell asleep.

☆   ☆   ☆

The next morning, Françoise and Tom were probably still asleep when I woke at ten. I got up an hour later and went to check my mail. Several envelopes, all from debt collectors. Just about every organization I'd ever had anything to do with was threatening to sue me. That was almost funny. If they were prepared to spend money on suing me for everything I had—which was nothing—I was happy to go to court and watch them go through it. I'd become quite fond of my long-term debts; it was kind of like a marriage.

I drank some hot water and spent a couple of hours on the phone trying to hustle some work and getting nothing. I was hoping to use the phone to get enough work to make enough money to keep the phone from being disconnected so I could keep on using it to hunt work. The cycles of existence.

I went out for a walk.

Françoise and Tom spent most of the day in bed, getting up only to make coffee, use the toilet and occasionally eat something. They fucked slowly, over and over. Françoise liked it, even though sex was always a disappointment for her. She preferred to fantasize. Tom was nervous and tried too hard, but she didn't really mind and she didn't let on.

In the late afternoon they drove to a restaurant near the theater. As they ate dinner she told him that she had no money and would have to find a job. He told her not to worry about it, just to take it easy for a while and let him take care of things.

They went to the theater. She watched as he put on his stage clothes and had his make-up applied. She'd never realized that male actors wore make-up. Then she sat in the auditorium and watched the show.

It was a good production. Françoise had always been bored by Beckett's work, but now she was seeing it done properly. The actors camped it up, cartoonishly overstating every physical movement and facial expression. It looked like an old silent film, maybe a Charlie Chaplin one. Tom was great. He could make the audience laugh just by looking at them, then turn the pathos into desperation. He was also as sexy as hell. Françoise felt herself getting wet, and remembered the first time she saw him.

After the show she waited for him in the bar. He came in with the other actors. He put an arm around her waist and kissed her cheek. He asked her what she thought of the show. She told him. They got drinks and sat down.

It was a remake of the night before. They sat in the bar and Tom chatted with the various people who wandered in and out. Benny England came and held court for a while. Françoise didn't tell him how much she'd liked his production.

She wanted to leave, but she didn't say anything. Since she'd done it the night before, she didn't want to be seen to force Tom to leave if he didn't want to. She wanted him to want to. But they stayed until the bar was about to close, then Tom suggested a club. A few people were enthusiastic. Françoise shrugged.

The club was called Bow Wow. On the way there they stopped at a pre-club bar where a few other members of Tom's club-going posse were hanging out. Tom gave one of them some money, and he handed Tom something small. "Okay, we're fixed," Tom told Françoise, handing her one of the tabs.

"What is it?" she asked.

"Ecstasy. Have you had it before?"

"Just twice. It was okay. I didn't like it that much."

"It was probably just MDA. Just hallucinogenic speed. Real ecstasy's MDMA. These are white doves, the real thing."

She shrugged again and washed the tab down with a mouthful of beer.

When they arrived at the club their posse numbered about a dozen. The doorman greeted Tom by name, asked him how the show was going and what he was doing next. Tom stood and talked with him for at least ten minutes. The others went into the club. Françoise waited with Tom for a while, then got bored and went inside.

The club was busy. The music was hard techno. Françoise could feel it slamming into her. She wasn't really into techno, but she knew she'd like it better once the ecky kicked in. She wondered if anyone actually listened to techno in the daytime, when they were at home and straight. She wondered if Tom did. She hoped not.

Tom came in. They danced. While she was dancing she felt the drug start to take effect. Everyone started to look better, and she needed to touch Tom and be touched by him. The music wasn't conducive to tactile dancing—which would have turned into something more like moshing—but every few minutes they stopped and hugged each other, heads together, the sweat on their faces mingling and smearing. She really got into dancing. The music was perfect for it. It still thumped violently against her, but she'd stopped resisting and was going with it. She imagined the music as the sea during a ferocious storm, with her floating, being tossed at random by the waves. But it wasn't a claustrophobic, drowning sensation. She didn't feel helplessly at the mercy of it, but rather part of it, part of the storm.

Tom left the dancefloor. He came back with a large glass of water. He drank half of it, then handed it to Françoise. She didn't feel thirsty, but she'd sweated a lot and she knew she was probably dehydrated and not feeling it because of the drug. When she put the glass to her mouth, her body sucked the water down.

She found herself thinking about Benny England, and wishing she'd been nicer to him. He probably wasn't a bad person, just insecure and desperate to impress, desperate to be admired. And he was probably lonely. He was so fat, he probably didn't have a lover. Maybe that was why he was so aggressive; maybe he was resentful. Françoise felt sorry for him. What had seemed like asshole behavior now seemed endearing. She wondered if he'd be nicer if he had someone who was nice to him. When she started to imagine being in bed with him without revulsion, she knew that the drug was now kicking in even harder.

She danced for a while longer, then didn't feel like it anymore. She was rushing and she felt like she wanted to sit down and talk. She asked Tom if the club had a chill-out room. It did. He showed her where it was, but he wouldn't come and sit with her. He wanted to carry on dancing.

At that point, I was just about to go to bed. I felt strange. Earlier that evening a young woman had come to look at a vacant room in the house. She'd arranged to meet the landlord there at seven-thirty. He didn't show up, and when she rang the front doorbell I answered it. I told her she could use my phone to call the landlord. She did and he wasn't home. I offered her a cup of coffee and she said okay. We sat and talked for a few hours. She had long brown hair and wore a quilted jacket over a long sweater that reached halfway to her knees. The house was very cold, and she shivered even though she kept her jacket on. The door to the vacant room was locked, but I told her that it was pretty much the same as my room. She said that she wasn't interested in renting it, that it was too cold. She told me her story. Her name was Helen and she had to find a cheap place to live because she'd lost her job. She told me how she'd once gotten pregnant and had a miscarriage, how her mother had Alzheimer's disease. I knew from the easy way she told me these things that we weren't going to be friends or anything else, that she didn't intend to see me again. At last she said, "I'd better go or I'll miss the last train. It was good to talk to you."

I wrote down my phone number. "Okay. Call me sometime if you'd like to meet up. Or just stop by."

"Okay," she said, but I knew she wouldn't, and I didn't really care whether she did or not. I had no idea why I'd given her the number.

I didn't know what I was feeling as I went to bed. There are a few stock words used to convey emotions: happy, sad, elated, scared, excited, depressed etc. The way I felt wasn't covered by any of them. It wasn't a good feeling, but that's all I can say about it.

☆　　　☆　　　☆

Françoise sat in the chill-out room. A woman asked her, "Are you grinding your teeth?"

"I don't know," Françoise said. "I didn't notice."

"I think you are. I heard you," the woman said. She was about Françoise's age, and seemed friendly. "There's some speed in the ecky. That's what makes you do it. Try to stop if you can. If you don't break the habit you'll be doing it all night."

"Okay, I'll try. Thanks." A minute or two later she realized she was doing it again and made an effort to stop, to resist the impulse.

"I'm going to get some water," the woman said. "Do you want some?"

"Yes, please."

The woman left. She was gone for quite a while and Françoise forgot about her, but eventually she returned with two glasses of water. She handed one to Françoise and watched her gulp it down. "You okay?"

"Yeah," said Françoise. "Thanks."

"Are you here by yourself?"

To explain would have required too much energy and focus, so Françoise just said, "Yeah."

"I'm going to go and dance. Do you want to come?"

"No, thanks. I feel like sitting here."

"Okay," the woman said, still a little concerned. "Will you be okay on your own? I feel bad just leaving you here."

Françoise smiled at her. "I'll be fine. Go and dance."

She didn't know how long she sat there for. She concentrated on keeping her mouth open, on not grinding her teeth. She imagined how stupid she must look, and she laughed. She was getting some interesting visuals. It wasn't like the sensory overload of an acid trip. This was more precise, more controlled. She wished Tom would come and sit with her. She needed to be touched, to be held. He didn't come. She remembered an article she'd read about an experiment that someone had done with newborn babies. Half of the babies were treated normally—fed, changed, kept warm, hugged, kissed. The other half received exactly the same treatment except for one detail—they were given no physical expressions of affection, no hugs or kisses. The former group thrived, but the latter became sick and actually seemed to be fading away and dying. When they too were hugged and kissed their health improved and soon became normal. Françoise felt like one of those babies. She wondered if she could live without ever being touched. Although she really didn't want to dance, she went to look for Tom.

He was dancing with the rest of the posse. When Françoise joined him he smiled at her and kept dancing, as though she'd just gone to the toilet for a few minutes. They danced without a break until the place closed, although Tom would periodically run off and then come back with enough water to keep the posse hydrated.

Afterwards, Tom wanted to drive home. Françoise said he was in no state to. Tom said that he always drove home from clubs, and that the ecky wouldn't impair his driving. When Françoise said she wouldn't get in the car with him, he gave in and hailed a cab.

They had a long, easy, loving fuck before they fell asleep. The ecky took away Tom's nervousness. He relaxed into what they did, and was much better than he had been earlier that day. He didn't make Françoise come, but he got her very close. As Françoise fell asleep, she was aware that she hadn't heard a single conversation all night.

My lack of money was getting beyond a joke. There were days when I couldn't have eaten if it hadn't been for a guy who lived in the room below mine. His name was Robert. He shared a room with his lover, Adam. They both had HIV. Since Robert had gotten sick he'd had to quit work. But he got bored easily. He wasn't into reading, and his interest in music went no further than camp disco anthems. There wasn't enough on TV to occupy him constantly. During the day, Adam, who wasn't sick yet, was out at work and Robert was alone. So Robert passed the time by canning food. He'd buy food cheaply in bulk, and can it: beans, soup, fruit cocktail. He'd also bake breads and cakes. He canned and baked much more than he could use. So, in the late afternoon, he'd knock on my door and hand me a bag full of cans and, sometimes, a loaf of bread or a cake. I'd brew tea and we'd sit and talk. He'd tell me about the state of his health, and about his fraught relationship with Adam.

Françoise felt like hell in the morning. So did Tom, but he was used to it. They had slumped from the ecstasy high and now felt exhausted and depressed. They drank some water, then fell asleep again.

Françoise didn't wake until around three in the afternoon. Tom was already up. He'd taken some speed to kick himself out of his stupor. He asked Françoise if she wanted some, and when she said she didn't he brought her coffee and toast. After she'd eaten she got up and took a shower. Tom came into the bathroom. He was horny and wanted to fuck but she didn't feel well enough to. She told him that she didn't think she'd do ecstasy again if the come-down was always this heavy. Tom said she'd get used to it, which made her uneasy.

They went out to dinner. They ate almost in silence, Françoise still feeling subdued and flat. Tom didn't say much, apart from telling her how much he loved her.

They went to the theater. Françoise watched the show again, then waited for Tom in the bar. When he came in with his entourage, Françoise started to feel that the play wasn't the only thing Tom repeated every night.

When the bar closed and Tom asked if anyone wanted to go to a club, Françoise said she couldn't handle it and just wanted to go home. Tom tried to persuade her, then gave up. When he nodded and said "Okay," she thought he was going with her. But he gave her money for cabfare and said he'd see her later.

At Tom's, for lack of anything else to do, she went to bed.

But she wasn't really tired. She got up and looked at the contents of his bookshelf. Mostly plays and books on theater, a couple on film. She picked out a history of the French New Wave cinema and read it in bed for a few hours.

She became tired eventually, but she still couldn't sleep. She felt like she was floating, like she had no life, no context, where she was.

She was still awake when Tom came home. It was four in the morning. He undressed and got into bed, then snuggled against her, the ecstasy he'd taken enhancing the feel of her nakedness against his. "You're so beautiful," he said. "I love you."

"Then why didn't you come home with me?"

"Are you pissed at me?"

"I don't know. I don't understand why you didn't want to be with me."

"I did. I just wanted to go to the club first. I knew you'd be here when I got home."

"Is that what you want?"

"What?"

"Me waiting at home for you like a good little girl?"

"No, I want you with me. I wanted you with me tonight, but you didn't want to come."

"Do you go to clubs every night?"

"Not every night. But most nights, yeah. That's my life."

"It's not my life."

"It can be if you want it."

"I don't want it. That's not how I want to live, Tom. I don't want to spend every night with a bunch of people I can't talk to."

"These 'people' are my friends."

"They're not mine."

"You don't like them?"

"No, I don't. I don't mind them either. I don't feel anything for them. There's no way for me to know them. They never talk with each other. My friends are people I can talk with and be close to, not people I just take drugs and go to clubs with."

"But that's what I do. There're people I've been friends with for twenty years, and I don't feel anywhere near as close to them as I feel to some people I've taken ecstasy with who I've only known for weeks and hardly talked to at all."

"That's not friendship."

"Yes it is. Ecstasy opens you up. You see through all the superficial bullshit, and once you've taken it you can't go back."

"Shit, you sound like someone in the sixties talking about acid. It's just a drug, Tom. You trip on it. You get high and have a good time. That's all. It doesn't change anything."

"It does. It changed me. Look at how fast it all happened between the two of us. That could never have happened to me before I started doing ecky."

"Then I'm just a drug trip. Why didn't you take acid and just hallucinate me?" She started to cry and turned away from him.

"Françoise." He put an arm around her. Then she felt his hard cock rubbing against her ass, trying to get between her legs.

"Don't."

"I want you." He turned her over so that she was lying on her back.

"Don't. I don't feel like it."

"You will." He began kissing her neck. She tried to stop crying and get into it but she couldn't. He was still kissing her, pressing his cock against her cunt, trying to get inside her, but she was completely dry. He stopped, finally seeming to notice the state she was in. "What's wrong with you? What're you so upset about?"

She turned away from him again, crying into the blankets. He got out of bed and left the room. She heard him go down the stairs. Then she heard the sound of a tap running. She pictured him sitting in the kitchen drinking tea or coffee.

All winter I had been thinking about a woman I used to live with. Not really her, but the details of that time. We lived out in the sticks, but we both worked in town. We'd get up in the morning and eat breakfast, arguing happily about whose turn it was to start the car. One of us would run outside, turn on the ignition as fast as possible, then run back inside and scarf some more food while the engine warmed up. Then we'd both run out to the car, cursing and laughing in the raw cold. We'd drive into town, to the work that waited for us there.

That scene had been playing in my head, over and over. Play. Rewind. Play again. It's playing again now.

Françoise fell asleep and didn't wake when Tom came back to bed. When they woke in the afternoon she said she wasn't going to the theater with him that evening. He nodded. He went to the bathroom and jerked off. He didn't know if she'd be into fucking him and, drug-free and in daylight, he was too embarrassed to ask her. He brought her some coffee in bed, then said he'd see her later and left.

She got up and took a shower. Then she went to the kitchen and looked in the fridge. A carton of milk, some cheese, a jar of pesto sauce, a can of beer. Nothing else. She sliced the cheese, found some bread in a cupboard and made a grilled cheese sandwich. She found a box of tea bags and brewed a pot.

However bright it was outside, every room in the house was always shadowy and dim. When she'd first seen it, Françoise had thought it pleasantly melancholy. Now it just seemed drab, almost squalid.

She had to get out, but there was nowhere to go. She remembered that there was a cinema across the road from the theater. She might as well go there, no matter what was showing. She had about twenty-five dollars left from the money she'd arrived with. That ought to be enough to pay for a movie, some food and bus fare.

She went out and knocked on the door of a neighboring house. The guy who opened it told her what she wanted to know about bus directions and schedules.

The bus dropped her near the cinema. She got lucky with

the movie—it was a martial arts adventure made in the early seventies and starring Jackie Chan. It was in Chinese, with English subtitles. Whoever had done the subtitling didn't seem to have studied English beyond high school. There were lines like *"You dirty guy! I'll take your teeth!"* that had Françoise cracking up along with everyone else.

The movie finished at around nine. Françoise drank a beer in the cinema bar. The bar served food, but it was expensive. Françoise ordered the cheapest item on the menu, a bowl of soup. She was still hungry after she'd eaten it. She decided to walk around and see if she could find a cheap place to eat.

As she walked past the theater, she saw Tom come out with his group. They all saw her and said awkward hellos.

"Hi," said Tom. "Where've you been?"

"I went to see a movie."

"Oh, right. What're you doing now?"

"I don't know. I'll get some food. Then maybe I'll go home."

"Okay. See you back there." He looked at the others. "All right, let's roll."

Françoise stood and watched as they walked away and got into cars.

She stayed standing there for some minutes after they'd driven away. Imagine a close-up of her face, her eyes wet and reflecting the night. Then maybe the camera pans, an aerial shot, her standing by herself on the streetlit sidewalk. None of this went through Françoise's mind as she stood there.

She walked. She didn't feel hungry anymore, but she was cold and her stomach was gurgling and she knew she'd feel worse if she didn't eat. She found a burger place and got a beanburger and fries and a Diet Coke. The burger was tasteless, but it was cheap and filling. She didn't want to be around people. She asked the guy who served her where the nearest park was. He said there was a hill nearby that was a kind of park; at least, it had grass and park benches.

She went there. You or I would have been too paranoid to go there at night, seeing a bearded, plaid-shirted axman behind every bush. But Françoise never thought that way. It never occurred to her that anyone might want to harm her, and it would be a long time before anyone did.

She sat on a bench in the dark and looked down at the town as she ate her food. Somewhere amongst all those lights Tom would be dancing in a club. She didn't know what to think about him. In a way she hated him, but she couldn't make enough sense of how he'd treated her to hate him with absolute conviction.

It got very cold. She couldn't face going back to the house, being there when he got home. So she stayed where she was. She lay on the bench and curled up, not to sleep, just to be warmer. It didn't make any difference. She thought about how strange it was, being on this hill in the dark in a city she didn't know in a country that wasn't hers. All her life, everywhere she'd ever been—at school, at work, in cafes, in bars, in her apartment—someone had always known she was there. There was always someone who could locate her. But no one knew where she was now. No one in the entire world knew she was shivering on this hill. But the cold knew, and the dark knew, and the benches and the trees and the bushes knew. They knew it all. She lay there for so long that they became familiar, as though they were more than objects and really had something to do with her.

The cold started her crying. She cried for as long as she could, then became bored. The boredom was the worst of it. She would never have believed that time could pass so slowly. She'd look at her watch, then force herself not to look at it again for a while. She'd wait for what seemed like a half-hour, then look and see that only about ten minutes had gone by. At first she thought there must be something wrong with her watch, but she counted to sixty as she peered at the second hand crawling round the face, and she realized that the watch was right. She wished she had a book with her, but it was too dark to see properly and too cold to concentrate.

Just before it got light, she was so cold that it was almost painful. She couldn't sit still. She jogged on the spot, feeling ridiculous. She threw punches at the air, imagining that she was aiming at Tom's benign, drugged, beaming face.

When the sky began to lighten, she walked down the hill. She liked the deserted streets of the town at that hour. She wandered around for a while, then went into an all-night diner and had coffee. Nothing had ever felt or tasted so good, the heat in her mouth and throat and stomach. The waitress refilled her mug twice. Françoise sat there for as long as she could have without ordering anything else. When she left she decided to walk to Tom's house. She was a little lost, so she knew it would take a while to find her way there.

The waitress who'd served Françoise had been working all night. Her name was Judith. Her shift finished at eight in the morning. She went home and slept for a few hours, then got up, showered, and made scrambled eggs and coffee. After eating, she went to visit her sister. As she waited for a bus home that evening, two men approached her. They spoke to her, she answered. They got angry at her answer, or they may have been angry all along. They didn't stop kicking her even after she'd passed out. Then one of them found a piece of broken fence post and hit her with it. A surgeon had to rebuild her face, using photos of her as his blueprint. But none of the operations managed to make her look like anything better than an ugly sister of the woman in the pictures.

Actually, that didn't happen. Yes, it did. It happened to a woman I knew long after I knew Françoise. But it seems appropriate to tell you about it the way I have. Because you should know about it. And even though Françoise never met the woman and wasn't around when it happened, it happened in the world she lived in, in a city she once passed through. Though oblivious to it, she was closer to it than she seemed to know. The remoteness, the separation, was only in her mind. And, the way her life ended, the separation disappeared.

Tom was in bed and asleep when Françoise got in. She didn't wake him. She went to the living room and fell asleep sitting in a chair, then woke a while later and moved to the couch. When she woke again she could hear Tom moving around in the kitchen.

She went to the bathroom, brushed her teeth and took a shit. Then she went to the kitchen. Tom was sitting at the table, drinking coffee. He looked at her and said nothing.

"I'm leaving," she said.

"I know."

"Do you know why?"

"No."

"Well, I don't know how to explain it to you. I've tried. You don't get it."

"No. I don't."

"Can I have some coffee?"

He poured it for her. "Are you going back to Holland?"

"No."

"Where'll you go?"

"I don't know."

"You don't have any money. What're you going to do?"

"Find a job."

"You can't work. You don't have a Green Card."

"Then I'll have to find someone who'll hire me without one."

"That won't be easy."

She laughed unhappily. "Surprise."

"You won't get a good job that way."

"Then I'll get a bad one."

"Where will you stay? You can't sleep rough."

"I did last night."

She went to the bedroom and packed her things. Tom asked if she wanted a lift somewhere. She said he could drop her in town, near the theater, since he was going that way anyway. On the way there he stopped at a bank, withdrew $200 from the cash machine and gave it to her. She put it in a pocket of her jeans. "Thanks."

As she got out of the car he told her, "Don't worry about paying that money back." She just nodded. The thought of paying him back hadn't occurred to her.

He sat in the car and watched her lift her bags out. He wanted to make some gesture of goodbye—tears, a final hug or kiss. But her face was as set as that of Anne Parillaud in *Nikita*. She hefted her rucksack, picked up her bag and gave Tom a quick nod before she walked away.

She ate in the diner she'd gone to the previous night. Then she went to the cinema, hoping it'd be showing a different movie than last night's. It was. She went in and watched Herzog's remake of *Nosferatu*. She'd seen it before, but for her it was a movie to which the law of diminishing returns didn't apply. This time its dark landscapes suited her mood as she thought of the hill that awaited her return.

FOUR

I had absolutely zero money. I'd almost failed to make my rent. The house had changed owners, and the new landlady was so fed up with my late payments that she'd have evicted me if I hadn't been able to pay in full and on time that month. I'd had to do some shoplifting, something I hadn't done in years. The store detective wasn't as good a store detective as I was a thief, and I got away with a batch of CDs. Even after I'd ripped the magnetic strips off them I still expected alarms to sound as I walked out the door. As soon as I was round the corner I started running, just through nerves. That night I managed to sell the CDs for enough to make up the shortfall in rent money.

But that left me without as much as a cent, and with the rent due again in a few weeks. I had some food in the cupboard, courtesy of Robert—some cans of soup and refried beans—but not enough to last more than a week. My phone bill had arrived, and it wasn't for a small amount. I had final demands for gas and electricity.

My shoplifting luck ran out. I was walking out of a store with three CDs tucked into my belt under my sweater when the store detective blocked my way. I shoved him and ran, but he came bounding after me and jumped on my back as I reached the sidewalk. I fell under his weight, ripping my jeans and scraping my knees. I squirmed under him, pushed him off and punched him in the face. He gasped and let go of me. I tried to stand up, but he grabbed one of my legs. I used the other to kick him in the face. He tried to crawl away from me, shouting for help. I aimed another kick at him, missed and fell against a parked car. I pulled the CDs from under my sweater and hid them behind a wheel. As I got to my feet two more of the store's employees appeared. My playmate got up and grabbed me again.

"Get your fucking hands off me!" I bawled, twisting away from him. He took a swipe at me, hitting me on the side of the head. One of his colleagues pulled him back. The other took me by the arm. "I'm fucking warning you—leave me alone, or I'll call the police," I told him.

The store detective was bleeding from his nose and a cut under one eye. "We're getting the cops anyway," he said. "He's got a bunch of CDs."

"I don't know what the dumb fuck's talking about. I haven't got anything. Let's go inside and you can search me," I said, wanting to get them away from the CDs. "I was just leaving the store and the fucking asshole attacked me."

They led me back inside the store. We went to a backroom and they searched me. Then they began to apologize. I said an apology wasn't enough, I'd been assaulted, publicly humiliated, and my clothes were ruined—my jeans were torn and there was blood on my jacket. I threatened to call the police, and said I'd definitely be talking to a lawyer.

They took me to see the manager. I left the store with a new pair of jeans and a hundred dollars in cash. I passed the car where the CDs were hidden, but I didn't dare stop and pick them up. I'd been afraid that one of the store staff would go out, look for a likely hiding place, and find them. Now I was too paranoid to take any chances.

The manager had been angry and worried, and as I walked home I enjoyed imagining what he might do to the guy I'd tangled with. Maybe he'd fire him. Maybe the guy would end up so desperate that he'd have to steal. The ache of my bruises and the sting of my scraped knees did nothing to make me charitable.

The money would get me some groceries. But what about the utility bills? And next month's rent? And what happened when the food ran out? I'd lost my nerve for shoplifting now. I'd been broke before, but this time it had lasted so long that I was afraid it wouldn't end. I remembered when I was seven years old, my mother leaving me in the playground while she begged in the street outside. I'd play on the swings and watch her speak to people passing by, watch some of them stop and give her a little money. It would have been easier for her if she'd kept me beside her, let them see that she had a child. But she wouldn't do that. She wouldn't put me through it.

I remembered watching her, and how it felt. And now I was nearer to being there myself than I'd ever thought I would be. I knew I couldn't go through it. I was too afraid of it.

The next morning I got up early and went out. I bought a paper, then went to a cafe and had breakfast. Then I poured coffee and opened the paper at the recruitment section.

This was the "quality" paper, and I knew it wouldn't advertise any jobs I was qualified for. I wasn't actually qualified for anything—I hadn't finished high school, and had no certificates at all. This paper didn't carry ads for dishwashers, which had been my main form of legitimate employment. But that wasn't what I was looking for now—it didn't pay well enough to bail me out of my present difficulties.

I scanned for a while, circling a couple of ads. Then I went home and called the numbers. One of the positions had been filled, but they were still taking applications for the other. I told a few lies over the phone and they sent me an application form. I told some more lies as I filled it out—in fact the only details I didn't fabricate were my name, address, phone number and date of birth. About a week after I delivered the form to their office, they called me and asked me to come for an interview.

I got the job. I wasn't surprised—if the claims I'd made had been true, I'd have been one of the best-qualified applicants. And my bullshit at the interview was so good I nearly convinced myself.

I'd never have gotten away with it had the employer been a private company, but the job was with the city and I had faith in bureaucratic ineptitude. They never checked my qualifications or experience, seeming satisfied with a forged letter from an imaginary previous employer.

The work itself was no problem, even though I didn't have a clue about any of it. My duties were mainly supervisory, and I'd figured that my underlings must know what they were doing. That's how it was—when they came to me with problems, I just listened to them, nodded thoughtfully as they discussed the options, then asked them, "What would *you* prefer to do?" Whatever the answer, I'd pretend to consider it, then say, "I think that'd be the best way." I found that, as well as getting away with not being able to find my own cock in the dark using two hands and a flashlight, I also became a popular supervisor. They thought I gave great advice because I told them to do what they wanted.

Aside from sharing my wisdom and doing some easy administrative stuff, there wasn't much for me to do. Most of the time I was being paid to sit in my office reading books and making personal phone calls. The irony was beautiful—when applying for dishwashing or waiting jobs I'd been given drug tests and checked for a criminal record, yet my first trip to the realm of the "professional" was obstacle-free.

The only down-side was that the job was temporary. It was only for six months. But that didn't really bother me; with six months of genuine experience, I shouldn't have much trouble finding something else.

A week or so after I'd started, I came home one evening and heard raised voices as I unlocked the front door. I stopped and listened. It was coming from upstairs, and one of the voices belonged to Pat, the landlady. She was arguing with Robert. Since he'd had to quit work and survive mainly on what Adam earned from his job in a supermarket, the rent was sometimes a problem.

"Robert, I do sympathize but I'm not responsible for your being sick," she was telling him.

"I know that. I'm not saying it's your problem. But the situation is—"

"The situation *is* that you pay your rent or get out. I don't want to hear any more excuses. I'll be back the day after tomorrow. I'll expect either the rent—in cash—or for your room to be cleared out."

As I was climbing the stairs she passed me on her way down. "Hi, Barry." She gave me a big, sunny smile, glowing with smugness and money. I nodded and walked past her. I wanted to grab her by the hair and smash her face into the wall, again and again, until bits of her were sticking to the wall, pieces of her teeth embedded in the dirty plaster. It wasn't so much her cruelty as her hypocrisy. She was a senior social worker, ran a Gestalt group from her home and was always ready to spout some New Age theory to anyone who'd listen.

But she evicted more people for being late with rent than any other dumplord I ever heard of. It didn't make sense. If you're a dumplord you have to accept that the people who rent your dump are going to be people with money problems or they'd be renting somewhere better.

She evicted Robert and Adam a couple of days later. I don't know where they went or what happened to them. They said they'd get in touch with me once they found a place, but if they did I never got the letter. Whatever happened, I'm sure they're both dead now.

I decided to get some revenge on Pat and live rent-free for a while. I didn't let on that I had a job, and I ignored her threats. Strangely, now that I didn't have to live in that place, living there didn't bother me anymore.

One weekend I flew to another city to visit a friend who lived there. He was wealthy. He'd dedicated himself to making money and it had worked out. Now he was married and had a kid. In the evening we stood on the porch of his huge house and looked at his lawns. His property. Suddenly the idea that he owned it seemed stupid to me. The house and the land would be there after he died. The land had always been there and always would. He was its temporary occupant, as transient as a guest in a hotel. The land wasn't owned by him. It was indifferent towards him.

✩   ✩   ✩

I got away without paying rent for two months. Not that Pat was prepared to give me as long as that—she told me several times to get out, but I laughed in her face. Rather than take it to court, she seemed to decide that it was best to let me stay and keep hassling me until I came up with the money.

I said I'd pay her everything I owed by the start of the following month. I didn't mention that I'd found another place, a fairly decent apartment in a crummy neighborhood. I'd arranged to move in at the end of the month. The only problem was that it was unfurnished. But that wasn't really a problem. The day before Pat was due to pick up her money, I hired a van and loaded it with all the furniture in my room. Then I kicked in the door of a vacant room and helped myself to its furniture. It was all stuff the previous owner had bought in thrift stores years ago, but I knew Pat would still hate having to replace it.

My phone service had been transferred and I'd arranged for my mail to be forwarded. I drove away leaving nothing but a pile of unpaid bills.

I'm not even sure about what I'm feeling right now. It's about Françoise, obviously, but it's not just about her. A minute ago I found myself thinking about a woman I knew a long time before I knew Françoise. Her name was Rachel. She was beautiful, but she wasn't into me. We became friends of a sort. It turned out that her ex-lover was a guy I knew, a would-be writer who was an absolute prick. One day she told me that she'd met him in the street the night before. "I hadn't had it for a while, so I ended up fucking him in somebody's back garden." I was hurt and jealous, but also excited by the idea of her doing that. All I feel now, though, is sad and frustrated. But why am I thinking about that as I cry for Françoise? Am I mourning for more than her, for something she represents to me?

I didn't miss my poverty. I didn't mind the job either. Since I wasn't really supervised, I didn't even have to stay in the office.

I could come in for a couple of hours in the morning, then say I had a meeting somewhere and go hang out with friends for most of the afternoon. When I was in my office, I spent most of the time working on a book I was trying to write. I was also reviewing films for a small magazine, so I'd often go out and catch a matinee, then come back to the office and write my review.

But such is my sloth that even being asked to appear at a certain time every morning began to seem like an unacceptable imposition. And I resented having to wear a collar and tie. I decided to live as frugally as I could, so that when the job ended midsummer I'd have enough saved to coast through to the winter before I needed another.

Françoise would usually wake around dawn. She'd get out of her sleeping bag and put her coat on, then sit on the sleeping bag as she pulled on her boots. She'd squat behind a bush and piss, feeling the cold biting at her, penetrating the crack of her ass. She never shat on the hill unless she really had to. She didn't like the idea of her shit lying around the hill she slept on. She'd wait until later when she could use a public toilet.

When she'd stowed her rucksack and bag out of sight, she'd walk down into town and go to a cafe or diner. Most days she'd buy a paper on the way and look at the job ads while she ate a bagel and drank coffee. She'd see jobs that she thought she could do. She'd call the numbers, and often she'd get as far as an interview. Some of them wanted to hire her, but when they realized that she couldn't work legally they told her it wasn't possible.

In the evenings she'd sit in bars or cafes and sometimes go to movies. The money Tom had given her was running low and she didn't know how she was going to get any more, so she only ate one meal a day and tried to make a beer or a cup of coffee last for at least an hour.

One night she dreamt that she was on a bus journey. The surroundings weren't familiar, but it must have been America rather than Holland because the driver had an American accent.

He stopped the bus in some remote place and told Françoise to get off.

"But this isn't my stop. This isn't anywhere."

"Get off."

"Why?"

"Because I don't like you. I don't want you on my bus."

She looked to the other passengers, but she couldn't see them anymore. She got off the bus and it drove away, leaving her there, nowhere.

There was a vegetarian cafe called Beans. The food was quite cheap and the portions were large, so Françoise usually ate there. She sometimes spent the whole day there. The counter staff got to know her. The place was supposed to be a co-operative, but really it was owned and run by James, a nervous man in his late thirties. He'd give Françoise free coffee, and sometimes glasses of red wine if she was there in the evening. One day he came and sat with her while she ate. She told him how she couldn't find a job, and why. He said she could work in the cafe.

She started the next day. It didn't feel very different than before, since she'd spent so much of her time there anyway. It was counter service, so the work was easy. It was more like hanging out, as she joked and talked with the customers and the other waitresses.

She became friends with James, sort of. She befriended him because she was looking for me. She didn't know me yet, hadn't met me, but it was me that she was looking for—someone to be her friend and help her and not want something back. She liked James, but she knew he wasn't me. That's why she slept on the hill even when he offered to let her stay at his place. Not because she was afraid of him or didn't trust him, but because she knew why he wanted to help her and she didn't want to be guilty of using him.

But she still spent a lot of time with him, often going for a drink with him on evenings when they weren't working. He didn't have any other friends. He told her that he hadn't had a girl-friend in more than three years. She could see why; he had an air of twitchy desperation that would put women off. But she couldn't think of a kind way to tell him.

One night he climbed the hill with some blankets, some food and a thermos full of coffee, fantasizing about spending the night there with her. But she was sleeping in the bushes and he couldn't find her. He searched for about an hour, then gave up and left. She never knew he was there, and he never told her or anyone else.

Another night they were sitting in a bar and she told him what had happened between her and Tom. He asked her how it felt when she was in love.

"I don't know. It depends."

"On what?"

"Different things. Whether the person is in love with me or not."

"How do you feel about me?"

"What do you mean? I like you, of course."

"Are you in love with me?"

She laughed, then realized he wasn't joking. "No," she said.

"I thought maybe you were."

"Why?"

"Because I'm in love with you."

She looked at her glass of wine on the table, smiled awk-wardly, didn't say anything.

"Are you attracted to me?" he asked her.

"No. I don't want that. What I need is friends."

"Do you think you ever could be?"

He wasn't making it easy. "No. I don't often like men that way. I like women better."

As they left the bar he said she could sleep on his couch. He always said that, and she always said no. He watched her walk away, towards the hill.

☆   ☆   ☆

"*Many men have loved the bells you fastened to the rain./And everyone who wanted you, they found what they will always want again./Your beauty lost to you yourself, just as it was lost to them.*" Leonard Cohen again. Françoise loved that song. It should be on the soundtrack of her movie.

In the cafe the next day, James completely ignored Françoise, aside from telling her what to do. The day after that, he gave her a written list of chores and didn't speak a word to her all day.

This went on for about a week. It was Françoise's habit to leave the cafe during her breaks, walk a few blocks and then come back. She usually told James she was going, but now she didn't feel able to say anything to him. So when it came time for her morning break she just left.

When she got back, James started on her before she was even behind the counter. The cafe was busy, but he didn't lower his voice or ask to speak to her in private.

"What do you think this is, Françoise? A kindergarten? You can't just walk out of here whenever you feel like it—"

"Yes, I can," she said, just as loudly. "I work here. I'm not a prisoner. I can walk out of here, or anywhere else, anytime I feel like it." She was so angry that she had to make a conscious effort to speak in English.

Some of the customers were looking embarrassed, and a few others seemed fascinated, but James wasn't letting it go. "You could have been needed here. It's only common courtesy to let me know when you're going outside."

"Since you haven't even said hello to me since I told you I didn't want to be your girlfriend, why do you want me to talk to you now?" James turned a pale red and said nothing. "If I have to sleep with you to work here and not be treated like a dog, just say so and I'll leave."

All conversation in the cafe had stopped. Not everyone was looking, but everyone was listening.

James said, "No, you don't have to leave."

Françoise walked behind the counter and put on her apron. For the next few hours James ignored her. The other waitresses ignored him.

On her afternoon break, Françoise didn't leave the cafe but sat at a table and looked at the accommodation ads in the paper. They were all too expensive.

James came over. "You don't have to stay here during your break," he said. "You can go outside if you want."

"I know. I can do anything I want."

He sat down. "I'm sorry about how I've been behaving. I know it was terrible."

"Okay."

"Am I forgiven?"

"Yeah."

"Are we still friends?"

She rolled up the paper and hit him lightly with it. "Stop being dumb. If you want to be helpful, find me somewhere to live."

She meant it as a joke, but he did it. When she showed up for work the next day he told her that someone he knew had a place for rent. It was a cottage outside town, an hour's bus ride away. "It's falling to bits, from what I hear," James warned her. "Living there would be one step up from camping. But it's cheap, and it's better than under a tree."

She went to look at it. It was in even worse condition than James had thought, but she fell in love with it. It was surrounded by trees and forest and had a river close by. And it actually had some furniture, which would save some expense. She moved in.

FIVE

There was a heatwave in August. Exhausted by the heaviness of the air, people sat in the cafe and tried to fend off the heat-crazed wasps that attacked them. There was an arts festival in town, and in the evenings when the wasps were placid there was live music in the cafe.

Françoise was working in the afternoon, looking forward to the evening when it would be cool and her work would be finished and she could sit and drink wine and listen to the musicians playing. I came in and waited in line at the counter. She noticed me as soon as I walked through the door. There was something about the way I looked, though she didn't know whether it was good or bad. Aged about thirty, skinny, dressed all in black that clashed shockingly with my dyed yellow hair. Glasses so geeky-looking that she wondered if that was why I'd chosen them. Jug ears, long pale face, huge brown eyes. She kept looking at me as she served the people in front of me. I noticed, smiled at her. She smiled back.

I asked for a pot of raspberry tea.

"Pardon?"

I repeated it.

"I don't think we have that. Have you had it here before?"

"No, I just saw it there." I pointed to the list of teas chalked on a board above the counter.

"Which one?"

"Second from the top."

"Oh, *rasp-berry*. I'm sorry. You speak very fast."

I laughed. "I know."

She saw me in the cafe again the next day, and the day after that. I sat writing in a little notebook. When she was clearing tables she came over and said, "Are you going to live here?"

"Uh-huh, I'm here a lot. I'm reviewing a lot of movies at

the festival. The Filmcenter's just up the road, so I come in here and write my reviews, then go and phone them in."

"Who do you write for?"

I told her. She nodded and went back to work. When it was time for her break she came and sat with me. "Am I disturbing you?"

"No, I'm just about finished."

"What film did you see today?"

"*Spanking the Monkey*."

"I want to go and see that. I've been too busy working here. Is it good?"

"Yeah, especially considering it's somebody's film school project." I offered her my notebook. "Here's the review, if you can read my writing."

She smiled, shook her head. "I wouldn't understand. My English isn't very good."

"Sounds good enough to me. Where're you from?"

"Holland."

"What's your name?"

"Françoise."

"Barry." I held out my hand and she shook it. We grinned hugely at each other. "How long've you been in the States?" I asked her.

"Four months."

"I know everybody probably asks you this, but what made you come here?"

"My boyfriend was American. I came to be with him, but I left him a week after I got here."

"Are you going to stay here for good?"

"I don't know. I'm not allowed to be here, so they might catch me and kick me out. And I won't have a job soon."

"How come?"

"This place is closing. It was going to close a while ago, but they decided to keep it open until the end of the festival. But when the festival ends, so does my job."

"You'll get another easily enough. There's lots of cafes in this town."

"I hope so. But I'm not allowed to work. I got a job here because the owner likes me."

"What'll you do if you can't find something?"

"I don't know. Something will happen. I'll be all right."

She really believed that. She once wrote in her diary, *"Good things always happen to me. When I have no money, I find wild mushrooms or someone feeds me. God blesses me."* She said she had no religion, but she still meant that.

A friend from New York came to stay with me for the last week of the festival. He was a filmmaker, and he came to the festival every year. This year we'd arranged to do a reading together at an arts cabaret in a gallery.

The show started at midnight, but Milt and I wouldn't be on until one. We sat in a nearby bar until 12:45, then went to the gallery. As we stood at the back and waited to be announced, I saw that Françoise was there. She was sitting on her own at a table near the front.

Milt and I went on and read a comical dialogue from one of his movies. Then I did a piece of my own, based on something I'd read in the paper about a guy who was so friendless that he'd invented a mechanical arm to give him a high-five when he was watching sport on TV and his team scored. The gallery was dark and I'm near-sighted, so I couldn't see the audience beyond the first row of tables. But I could see Françoise laughing, her face shining darkly in the candlelight.

When the show was over and people were just sitting around drinking and talking, I looked for her. But she was gone.

"Did you see the woman sitting at the table front right?" I asked Milt.

He hadn't. He'd been wearing dark glasses on stage and hadn't been able to see a thing.

"Tomorrow we'll go to the cafe where she works and I'll introduce you," I told him. "She's the most gorgeous woman you'll ever see."

Milt looked interested. He had the worst luck with relationships I've ever heard of. It was baffling, because he was a great guy and not bad-looking, but it just didn't happen for him. He told me how ironic he thought it was that, now that his movies had become ultra-hip, so many people he knew in New York were spitefully envious of him. "I never wanted to be famous, I was just doing my work. They all dream of being famous, and I dream of having a girlfriend."

The next evening we went to the cafe. There was no sign of Françoise. I went to the toilet and, as I came out of the men's room, she came out of the women's.

"Hi," I said. "I saw you at my gig last night."

"Yes. You were...joyful."

I didn't correct her, deciding that it wasn't the time for an English lesson. "Thanks. I looked for you afterwards but you weren't around."

"No. I stayed with a friend in town, and I didn't want to be very late and wake her up."

"Are you working tonight?" I asked, noticing that she wasn't wearing her apron.

"No. I've finished for today. I'm just relaxing now. There's a jazz band playing soon."

We went and sat at my table. Milt almost started drooling. "Françoise, this is my friend Milt," I said.

"Yes, I saw you last night, too," she told him as they shook hands.

We drank wine and talked. A book of Milt's filmscripts had just been published, and he had a copy in his bag. He tried to impress Françoise by showing it to her. She looked at the cover, smiling at the photo of him. Then she began flipping through the pages. She read for quite a while. I tried to talk with Milt, but the sight of her reading his stuff made him too nervous to focus.

She finally handed the book back to him. "You're a good writer, but I don't like it," she said.

"Oh?" He was so into her that he didn't mind what she said, just as long as she was talking to him. "Why's that?"

"You don't seem to like women." Milt looked confused, and I could understand why. He liked women, all right. He liked women a lot. "All these jokes about how the guy can't get a girlfriend, it seems like you're blaming the women for it. You never show how the women feel."

"Yeah, you're probably right," Milt said, just going along with her.

"You're totally wrong," I told her. "Maybe it's because it's not in your first language, but you're just not getting it. Blaming the women doesn't come into it; the men are making fun of themselves for not being able to get laid. You have to judge a movie in terms of what it's about, not in terms of what you want it to be about. It'd be pointless for Milt to deal with how the women feel. That's not what his movies are about. The men don't understand how the women feel. That's why they can't figure out why the relationships turn to shit."

"Yeah," Milt said. "I'm not blaming anybody. I'm just being funny to keep from being bitter. Kind of laughing to keep from crying." He looked at me. "Thanks, dude. I always wondered what my movies were about. I should have gotten you to write the blurb for the book." All three of us burst out laughing.

She told me later that this was the point at which she'd decided she really liked me. "I never really get to be friends with men. It's not that I don't like them, it's that they never talk with me properly. They just sit there and look at me and nod their heads and don't listen to what I say. They just agree with me so I'll like them. When you started arguing with me, I knew you'd be my friend."

I grew to understand what she meant. She couldn't get a conversation out of a man. One night I was in a bar with her and James. She was a little bit drunk, and she said she thought the reason that people committed suicide was curiosity to see what awaited them. I could hardly believe she'd say anything so crass and stupid, but James nodded and said, "Yeah, definitely." Afterwards I told her she should suggest that the earth was flat and see whether James agreed with that as well.

Why am I doing this? To keep Françoise alive?

Françoise left the cafe soon after the music finished, saying that she had to get the last bus home. She was leaving town early in the morning and would be gone for two weeks. It was her twentieth birthday in five days' time and she wanted to spend it alone, walking and camping in the mountains. The cafe would have closed down by the time she got back, so I wouldn't be able to contact her there. I asked her to give me her number so we could stay in touch.

"I don't have a phone," she said. "But I'll give you my address."

"Okay. And I'll give you my address and number." I wrote it on a page in my notebook, tore it off, handed it to her. She took the notebook from me and wrote in it, then gave it back to me. Then she said goodnight to Milt, winked at me and walked out of the cafe.

Milt and I smiled at each other. "What did she write?" he asked me.

I looked. Under her name and address she'd written, *"I look forward to seeing you. Was it just because of having a chat about our different feelings about films? Love, Françoise."*

I still have that notebook, full of scribbled film reviews and Françoise.

Milt stayed for a few days after the festival ended, just enjoying the quiet and the slow restoring of order after all the fuss and noise and egos. Then he went back to New York and I went back to my life.

I'd stashed enough money from my job to live on for a few more months if I was thrifty. The job had finished a few weeks ago and I was glad to be free again. I went on reviewing movies and working on my book, but I kept away from people. I was asked to do some readings, and I turned down all but the ones that paid well. I sat in the thick warmth of bars reading books and magazines. In the evenings I walked for miles. I left the answering machine on and didn't answer the doorbell.

One evening I was sitting in the cafe of the Filmcenter, waiting to go in and see a movie, when a hand ruffled my hair. Françoise.

"I knew I'd see you today," she said. "I just got back today, and I knew I'd meet you."

"Fate for sure. How're you doing?"

"Good." She was carrying a rucksack and tent. She heaved them off her shoulders and onto the floor, then sat on the edge of my table. "I'm tired, though. And I need to have a shower."

"So why aren't you at home?"

"The guy I hitched a ride with was coming into town. Not many people drive to my place. I'll get the bus home. But first I wanted to see my photographs. Have you seen them?"

I didn't know what she was talking about. Seeing my bewildered expression she said, "On the walls in here," and I got it. The cafe always had exhibitions of paintings and photos on its walls. There were two pictures of Françoise among the current exhibits. They weren't great; they took the warmth out of her loveliness and gave her the coldness of sculpted marble.

"Who took the pictures?" I asked.

"A guy who used to come into Beans. I'm quite angry about it, because he never asked me if he could use the pictures, and he never paid me anything. I don't mind, but he should have asked."

☆　　　☆　　　☆

I feel I might be betraying her by recording this story, since she never gave me her permission and can't now. There's a sense of guilt as I move this thin black pen over the ruled white pages of this notebook. But I'm doing it anyway. And, like the guy who took the pictures, I'm doing it for myself, not her.

"What are you doing?" she asked me.

"Going to see a movie."

"Are you reviewing it?"

"No. It's not a new release. But it's one of my favorites. *Love and Human Remains*."

"I'd like to watch it with you."

"Come on, then."

"No. I'm tired and I smell. I must go home."

"Well, call me and let's get together."

"I will. Would you like to come out to my place sometime?"

"Yeah. When?"

"Whenever you like."

"How about tomorrow? Or do you need time to get settled in again?"

"Tomorrow would be good. Can you come at around noon?"

"Yeah. No problem."

"Okay." She hauled her rucksack and tent back onto her shoulders. "I'll see you then. It's really beautiful out there."

That night I was so excited I couldn't get to sleep until close to sunrise. Things had taken such a turnaround for me in the last few months. I wasn't living in squalor anymore, and I could eat properly. And for Françoise to be interested in me...I didn't know where my life was going, but I knew that it was no longer where it had been, and I was glad.

I didn't hear my alarm clock at nine. I woke at eleven, too late to have any chance of being at Françoise's in an hour's time if I waited for a bus. I called a taxi company and asked how much it would cost to get a cab out there. Fuck it. I told them to send one round.

It was just as well. It turned out that her place wasn't in the village, but about a mile outside it, on the other side of some woods. It'd have taken me forever to find it on my own. The taxi driver took me as far as he could before the dirt road narrowed to a path. I paid him, got out and walked for about five minutes, out of the woods and past a couple of fields with cows grazing in them. I came to what I first thought was a ruined cottage, then realized it was Françoise's.

I knocked on the door. She opened it about a minute later, hair tangled, eyes squinting against the sunlight. "Hi." She smiled groggily. "Come in. I just woke up."

"Sorry I woke you."

"No, it's fine. I meant to get up hours ago, but I was more tired than I thought."

The cottage had one main room, plus a small kitchen, a shower-room and a toilet. The main room had two faded armchairs and an electric heater. There was a bed in the far corner.

I sat in an armchair. Françoise went into the kitchen to put on water for coffee. She came back and sat on the edge of the bed. She combed her hair with her fingers and shook her head, trying to wake up. "I drank too much wine last night," she said. She was wearing a navy blue tank top and red shorts. She was barefoot. Even then, just out of bed, tired and hungover, she was improbably lovely. You could have taken her picture right then and featured it in *Elle* or *Vogue* or *The Face*.

"Did you go to a bar after you left the Filmcenter?" I asked.

"No. I drank it here. I have a little red wine most nights." She stood up. "Do you want coffee?"

"Have you any tea?"

"No. I don't like tea. I should have remembered to get some—you always drank tea in Beans. We can walk to the village and get some."

"That's okay. I can drink coffee. But after that let's go into the village and I'll get you lunch. Or breakfast, in your case."

"Great! Thanks."

She made coffee. We went outside and sat on a bench in her garden while we drank it. She told me some of her story. I listened. It was a glorious late summer day, and all of it was in her face.

"Can I kiss you?" I asked her.

"Are you teasing, or do you mean it?"

I put an arm around her shoulders. "I mean it."

She smiled, not looking at me.

"Can I kiss you?"

Still smiling—the same awkward smile she'd shown James—she shook her head. "I know you want to," she said.

"But you don't?"

She shook her head.

"Okay." I took away my arm. "Forget I said it. I thought maybe you were into me, but obviously I was wrong. Let's be friends, anyway."

She looked at me, and now there was no awkwardness in her smile. "We already are."

She put on jeans and socks and boots and we walked to the village. She knew a shortcut through some fields that got us there quickly but got my black jeans and polished boots splattered with mud. Her jeans and boots were already muddy and she didn't care.

The village was really just a few streets. It had one little cafe that was also a store. But we were both vegetarians, and the menu was based entirely on meat. "Tell you what," I said. "Let's buy some food, take it back to your place and cook it." She was into that, so we went into the store and I bought some pasta, pesto sauce, vegetables, tea and two bottles of red wine.

Back at the cottage, I cooked the pasta and added the sauce while she chopped and fried the vegetables. We sat down to eat in the main room. As Françoise poured the wine I put my hands together and mouthed a quick grace.

I didn't expect her to notice, but she did. "Are you a Christian?" she asked.

"No. I'm not really religious at all. But I always give thanks for food, to whoever or wherever it came from. I'm always grateful to eat."

"Me too," she said, and she wasn't kidding. She practically inhaled her food. Her plate was empty before I'd even made an impression on the contents of mine.

"You must be starving," I said.

"Yes. I haven't eaten anything for two days."

"Seriously?"

"Yes."

"How come?"

"I don't have much money left. Just enough for my rent."

"Why didn't you tell me you were hungry?"

"It's not your fault. You didn't make me hungry."

"What's fault got to do with it? You can't go without food."

"I can for a while. Till I find a job and make some money."

"What if it takes you a while to find a job? And you won't get paid straight away."

"I'll be all right."

"I can lend you some money meantime."

"No. You're not rich either."

"Richer than you. I can lend you a little."

"No. I'll be all right. If you make me take it I won't spend it. I'll just keep it until it's time to pay it back."

"I thought we were friends."

"We are. I don't want to mess it up by letting you lend me money."

"What would you do if I was hungry?"

"I'd feed you."

"And if I refused your help you'd be angry."

"Yes," she admitted.

"Okay, let's compromise. Let me buy you some groceries. And anytime I'm here, which I hope will be often, you cook dinner for me."

She laughed. "All right. Thank you."

We went back to the village store. It was lucky that I had my checkbook on me. We walked back to the cottage laden with bags, so many that we couldn't climb fences to take the shortcut, and so we had to go the long way.

We dropped the bags on the kitchen floor, then went and sat in the armchairs and drank more of the wine. "This is all I need," she said. "When I don't have any money, sometimes I can live on coffee and wine."

"That's so bad for you. It can make you hypoglycemic or something."

"It's all right as long as I relax. If I have to go into town and do things, it can make me feel dizzy. But if I just stay here and don't waste energy it's all right."

A little later I said I'd better go, and asked her to show me where the bus stop was. "Okay," she said. "But you can stay the night here if you want."

"Yeah. I'd like to."

"Good. Do you want to take a walk in the woods before I make dinner?"

"It's getting dark."

"We'll stay on the path. I know the way. I walk in the woods a lot at night."

"Okay."

By the time we'd finished the bottle of wine we were on, it was completely dark outside. There was a moon, but I still couldn't see anything as we walked from the cottage, except for the looming trees and Françoise's silhouette in front of me. She said she could see perfectly, and she took my hand and led me around rocks and stumps that would have tripped me. We walked down the path into the woods, not saying anything. My eyes adjusted and I could see better. As we walked past a field, I breathed in a hot stench and then realized that it was coming from a huge bull that was standing near us, on the other side of the fence, pissing. The piss jetted out in a steaming torrent that lasted for minutes. Françoise and I just stood there and watched. She was laughing.

As we walked back to the cottage under the big, wild drifting of the moon, I was grateful to be there with her, to have the perfect essence of her there beside me, grateful to everything.

I'm not even sure what I mean by that. Though I'm beginning to see what I'm doing with these memories, this text. I'm looking for Françoise, trying to find her somewhere amongst it all, somewhere between the lines. And I'm not finding her. I'm afraid that she's not there. And I know she's not anywhere else.

We sat up and talked until after three in the morning, finishing the wine and chasing it with coffee and tea. I asked her what she planned to do if she was able to stay in the US long term. She said she'd like to go to film school. "I would like to be an actress, but my accent is impossible. So if I can't be in films I'd like to make them."

Drunk and exhausted, we went to bed. I'd offered to sleep on the floor, but she said it was okay. I wore a T-shirt and underwear, she wore her tank top and shorts. It was a narrow single bed. The feel of her legs against mine made my cock hard. I put an arm around her. She let me hold her but she didn't respond. After a while she murmured, "I can't sleep like this, Barry." I let go of her and she turned away.

The night after I heard the news about Françoise, I dreamt about her. I was lying on a bed and she was sucking my cock. I was wearing a bathrobe which she'd pushed up around my waist. As I got more and more excited, my ass suddenly pushed out a turd. It didn't squeeze out, but dropped out all at once. Françoise didn't notice. I pushed her off me, said I had to go to the toilet and, carrying the shit in my robe, I ran out of the room.

SIX

She went to see someone at the art school, and they gave her a job as a nude model for the life-drawing class. The pay was surprisingly good, better than anything she'd had before. But she didn't get paid until the end of the month, so for the first month she had nothing. She searched the woods for wild mushrooms, which she ate raw or fried in butter. A couple of times she took bags of them into town to sell to a restaurant. She wasn't sure whether the chef/owner really wanted the mushrooms or just wanted her. When she came in he would act like a nervous schoolboy, talking nonsense, dropping things and tripping over his own feet. As well as paying her for the mushrooms, he'd give her a meal and a glass of wine.

When she ran out of food she didn't tell me. I had to ask. When she admitted that she had nothing, I got her some more groceries. She still wouldn't take any money, even when I said she could give it back to me when she got paid. "I would take it from anybody else. Money isn't a big thing with me, but everybody gets uptight about it. I know you don't care so much, but I still don't want to take it. You and I shouldn't owe each other things." I couldn't see the difference between buying her food and just giving her the money. I said it was her who was being uptight, and that money obviously was a big thing to her, but she wouldn't change her mind.

But she said she wanted to give me a gift to thank me. She showed me a pile of glossy black and white photos of her and told me to pick any ones I wanted. That sounds like narcissism, but it wasn't. She was aware of her beauty, but not in a smug or conceited way. She was aware of it as a craftsman is aware of the quality of his product and his own skill in making it. She knew that her beauty was something that people wanted, something that it felt good to look at. She knew its quality, and her gift to me of the photos was an act not of narcissism but of generosity.

One night I went out to her place with my guitar. She'd told me that she'd written some songs, and I was curious to hear them. When I got there I found her reading an article about Tom in a film magazine. The magazine had come out the previous week. I'd bought it and read the article, but had decided not to mention it to Françoise.

"Listen to this shit," she told me. "'*Quinn has now all but renounced political activism, declaring that it simply leads to dead ends. His energy is now channeled through his passion for rave culture. "A lot of the fight had been knocked out of working class youth and replaced with apathy," he says. "But I'm seeing a revival of that vibrancy on the rave scene. The rave culture is so underground. It's existed for years and it still hasn't been co-opted by the establishment. I think that nowadays involvement in rave culture is probably the most real and effective form of political activism."*' Shit," Françoise said, closing the magazine. "That's so false. And so arrogant. How is dancing and taking drugs a political act? How is it going to help other people? He doesn't even believe it. He just can't admit that he's too busy having a good time to do anything important anymore."

I grinned. "I know. Rave's got a lot to answer for. I know a friend of Tom's who used to be a good writer. Since he discovered ecky, he can't get through a poem without mentioning Timothy Leary at least once."

She laughed and poured me some wine. "Maybe we should declare that sitting up all night drinking wine is political."

"Yeah," I said. "Set up our own party and run for election." When we'd stopped laughing I said, "Does the fact that you're so pissed off mean that you're still pretty hung up on Tom?"

"No. I don't care for him anymore. I'm just angry that he's so dishonest. He said he loved me, and it's obvious that he didn't. Especially since it's obvious that you do."

☆   ☆   ☆

I was about to try to convey her voice, reproduce the inflections of her speech. Like how she sounded the *h* in *honest*. But that's just a detail, a mannerism. Just information. What I want is to reproduce the sound of her voice, and that's impossible. I'm not even sure that I really remember her voice. I remember all the details, all the information. I can describe it using adjectives. But I can't hear her voice in my head anymore. When I try, I just conjure a female voice speaking with a sort of generic cartoon Teutonic accent that could be Dutch or German or something else.

"Yeah, I love you for sure," I said.

"But you're not in love with me?"

"No, not at all."

"Good. I'm not in love with you either, so that would be bad. Are you happy just being my friend?"

"Yeah. As long as you don't mind that I sometimes think about you when I jerk off."

She laughed. "No, I'm honored."

My money was running worryingly low, so I started looking for a job. I turned up a few that I could probably have talked my way into, but I didn't really fancy any of them. I was standing by my phone, debating whether to call any of them or hold out for something better, when it rang. I picked it up and heard Françoise crying. She said she was in the Filmcenter cafe and asked if I'd meet her there.

"Of course I will. But what's wrong? Has something happened to you?"

"I'll tell you when I see you. Come as soon as you can."

When I got there she was sitting at a table with a pot of coffee. She'd stopped crying. Somehow the authorities had found out that she was in the country illegally. She thought they may have been tipped off by a guy at the art school who'd asked her for a date and hadn't liked being turned down. She'd been given thirty days to leave the US or be deported.

"What're you going to do?"

"I'm going to go. I'll go back to Holland. I could just move house and avoid them for a while. But if they find me and I get deported I'll be banned from coming back for ten years. I don't want to risk that. I want to come back next year, if I have enough money."

"Have you enough to get back to Holland?"

"I still have the return ticket I came with. It's open. I think it's a little out of date, so I'll probably have to pay something. But not much. It's a pity I want to come back—if I got deported I'd get a free flight."

"How do you feel about it?"

Her eyes got wet. "I'm sad. I like it here. I like my job and I love my house. And—" She smiled as she cried. "I love my best friend."

Straining to keep my voice from shaking, I said, "Listen. Try to stop crying. Or I'm going to start as well."

She got hold of herself. "Okay. Do you know any men's hairdressers?"

"You mean like barbershops?"

"Yes."

"Yeah. Why?"

"I'm going to get my hair cut to cheer myself up. I'm going to get my head shaved."

"Seriously?"

"Yes."

I looked at her, imagining it. "Yeah, it'd probably look good on you. Well, you can save your money. I've got a barber's shaver, from when I used to shave my own head. I'll do it for you if you like."

"That'll be fun. I want to have fun while I'm still here. I don't want to be sad. I'll try to wait till I'm back in Holland and then be sad."

We went and saw the movie that was showing that afternoon,

Butterfly Kiss. It was about two psychopathic lesbians driving across Britain killing people. One of them was looking for someone but she never found her. She'd go up to strangers and ask if they were her. But they never were.

In spite of my cash shortage, I decided to lay aside the job hunt until Françoise had gone. I wanted to have time to spend with her. Then Milt called me from New York. An arts center there was putting on a season of performance art, and he was scheduled to give some talks and readings at it. But the movie he was working on was at a crucial stage and he couldn't take time away from it. He'd recommended that the organizers invite me to take his place, and they'd agreed. Although I was nowhere near as well-known as he was, his following would know me. And, if they were disappointed at not hearing him speak, at least I could talk about him from personal knowledge. The money was good. I had to be in New York for a week, starting two days before Françoise left the country. I said I'd do it.

A Sunday evening. Françoise sat cross-legged on her floor, surrounded by spread-out newspapers to catch the falling hair. A towel was tucked into the neck of her T-shirt. I stood over her, the shaver in my hand humming electronically. I finished and switched it off.

I wiped her head and neck with a paper tissue. "Okay, you can look now." I'd told her she wasn't to look in the mirror until it was done. Now she jumped to her feet and ran to the toilet to look.

"Yes! I like it!" she called. So did I. It was the perfect look for her. It highlighted her cheekbones and the set of her eyes and made her look like a glamorous space alien. She came over to me and I ran a hand over her head, feeling the soft fuzz that was still there. "Thanks," she said, and kissed me quickly and lightly on the lips.

"You can keep the shaver," I said. "It's quite easy to shave your own head, once you get the hang of it. I used to do my own."

As usual, we sat up late with the wine, in armchairs facing each other in front of the electric heater. I asked her what she planned to do when she got back to Holland.

"I don't know. I haven't thought about it. I'm not going to think about it until I'm there. I'm just pretending that it's not going to happen."

"Let me hear you sing," I said. My guitar had been at her place since I'd brought it there a couple of weeks before.

She picked up the guitar. "What do you want to hear?"

"The song about Lotte." She'd played it for me once and I hadn't been able to get it out of my head.

She played it now. The guitar part was slow and very rhythmic, almost gothic. She sang in a sweet, cracking voice, her monotone unable to reach the higher notes. There was enough love in her to break my heart.

"Tell you what," I said when she'd finished. "You can keep the guitar."

She just looked at me, smiling.

"I hardly ever play it these days," I said. "And I'd never be as good as you if I practiced for a decade. I've thought about selling it sometimes, but I couldn't bear the thought of it going to somebody I didn't know, who might not look after it. But I know you will."

"I'd love to have it. But you can have it back any time you want."

"It's yours. Play some more." She did, a couple of her own songs and one by Leonard Cohen. Then we went to bed.

I don't know why it happened, why she did it. As usual, she wore shorts and a tank top. I wore a T-shirt and underwear. As usual, we lay in each other's arms, cuddling. But usually we did that partly from affection and partly to warm ourselves. And usually we'd break after a few minutes, turn away from each other and sleep.

This time the embrace felt different, and we didn't break it. I stroked her back. Her T-shirt wasn't tucked into her shorts, and I touched her bare skin, feeling her muscles and bones. I lightly kissed her neck. She just lay still with her arms limply around me. I went on kissing her neck, using my tongue now. Her breathing deepened a little. She let me kiss all over her neck and face, but not her mouth. When I made to touch her tits, she stopped me and said, "I can't do this, Barry."

"Why not?"

"I'm afraid. When I sleep with men I get haunted by it. It's like I'm sick. I get obsessed, like a fever."

"Okay."

We just lay there for a while, holding and touching each other. At some point we began pressing and rubbing against each other. I began kissing her again. When I slipped my tongue into her right ear she moaned a little. I pulled off my T-shirt. She let me take off her vest. I pushed her arm above her head and licked her armpit. I'd never been into that with anyone else. I don't know why I wanted to do it with her, or why I liked it. I liked the taste and the smell of slightly ripe sweat on the moist hairs. Then I went back to licking her ear, imagining that it was her cunt. She shuddered and held me tight.

When I tried to get my hand inside her shorts, she said, "Just take them off." I did, amazed by the length of her legs as I pulled the shorts down over her ankles. I tried to get my face between her legs but she stopped me. "Don't. I just finished my period. There might still be some blood."

"Wouldn't bother me."

She laughed. "I know." She pulled me to her and turned her head to one side, wanting me to kiss her ear again. As I did, she pushed my pants down. My cock slid into her.

It wasn't a great fuck. She was so gorgeous that I couldn't get over it. I couldn't relax and go with it, and I'd wanted her so much and for so long that I couldn't distance myself from it and keep control. Though I tried to go slow, it couldn't have been more than thirty seconds before I came. I pulled out of her and sprayed all over her stomach and midriff.

She laughed breathily as I collapsed on top of her. "Sorry," I said.

"Don't worry."

I felt the sticky liquid gluing our stomachs together. "God, I can't believe how much I came."

"You were saving it up for weeks."

We both laughed. I lay beside her and put a hand between her legs.

"It's okay," she said.

"Are you sure?"

"Yes. It was good. I feel good. It doesn't feel good with men usually, but it does now."

She wrote in her journal, *"We were in bed and I knew he wanted to make love to me. But I didn't really. When I looked at him I wasn't excited, it was just Barry Barry BARRY BARRY BARRY. But I fucked him and it was nice. He found how sensitive my right ear is. How did he know that so soon? The other one isn't, and he didn't touch it. I felt good after it. No fever. I hope I didn't hurt him by moving away from him. I don't like to be cuddled after it. I know most people do. I think he does.*

"I also hope he isn't hurt when I tell him I don't want to do it again."

She had a going-away party a few days before she had to leave. It was in the back room of a bar, the same place where she'd once entered the songwriting competition. Quite a few people came along—students from the art school, people who'd worked with her at Beans. And James, of course.

I got really drunk. At the end of it all Françoise and I got a taxi to my place. I went to the toilet, tried to vomit, didn't manage to. Françoise helped me undress and get into bed. She asked me where my sleeping bag was. I told her and she went and got it. We hadn't shared a bed since the night we'd fucked. She laid out the bag on the floor just beside my bed. I said she could have the bed and I'd take the floor. I was drunk enough to sleep comfortably on broken glass. She said no, she liked camping on the floor sometimes. When she was tucked into the sleeping bag, she reached up to the bed, took my hand and pulled it down to her. She kissed it, then tucked it against her chest, just under her chin. I fell asleep.

I didn't wake until the afternoon. Françoise wasn't there, but she'd left a note on the sleeping bag.

Dear Barry,

I got up and made coffee and toasted a bagel. I was going to wake you up, but you need to sleep. I'm going to the Filmcenter for lunch. Have a nice slow wakening, and come there and meet me if you want to.

love,

F.

I drank a couple of pints of water to ease my hangover, then thought about Françoise as I jerked off. Then I got dressed and walked to the Filmcenter. It was after three, so there was a good chance that she wouldn't be there, but the walk would do me good.

She was there, sitting reading a *Love and Rockets* comic book. "I hoped you'd come. Does your head hurt?"

"Yeah." I sat down and theatrically rested my head on the table.

"Do you want some coffee?" She laughed. "Or would aspirin be better?"

"Coffee. Yeah. Gimme."

She laughed again and kissed the top of my head. Then she went to the counter and came back with a pot of coffee and a croissant. "Eat this. You'll feel better." As I ate, she said, "Do you want to do something tonight?"

"Yeah, if you do. Any ideas?"

"I don't feel like a movie. Are there any bands playing?"

"Claire's got a gig. Her band and three others. Don't know if the others're any good."

"Let's go anyway."

The gig wasn't until ten. We walked around for a while, then went and had dinner. As we came out of the restaurant we ran into James. He suggested going for a drink. I said I had some things to do, and arranged to meet Françoise in a bar near the venue a half-hour before the gig.

I went straight to the bar. I bought a paper on the way, and read it as I drank orange juice and lemonade. The following day and night would be the last I'd spend with Françoise. I had to leave for New York the day after.

I remember looking at her as we walked from the bar to the venue. Her shaved head. Red lips. Her long coat with the fake fur collar.

After the gig we went to a club. All the time I danced with her I had to make an effort not to stare into her face. Now I wish I had. It felt so good, I wish I'd recorded some details.

She stayed at my place that night. Neither of us had drunk much, and we got up at around nine. She went to get a bus out to her place. I had to pack for my New York trip. I was planning to go to Françoise's that evening, stay over, and go straight from there to the airport in the morning. Before she left my place I told her to look at my bookshelves and help herself to any books she liked that she thought might be hard to find in Holland. She took a few. One was a book of film theory by David Mamet, another was a biography of Sonic Youth. I don't remember what the others were. I re-read those two when I heard about Françoise, but it didn't make any difference.

☆   ☆   ☆

I bought a half-gallon tub of chocolate ice-cream on the way out there. She didn't have a fridge, so we had to leave it outside until we were ready to eat it.

We cooked a meal, drinking a bottle of wine as we did. Then we ate it, and pigged out on the ice-cream afterwards. We sat, bloated, by the heater. Our only light came from some candles on the coffee-table. We talked, and we both cried. We made plans for the future, for her to come back to the States, for me to go to Holland.

I finally said I had to get some sleep. She told me to go ahead, she wouldn't be long in following. I went and brushed my teeth, then came back and undressed and got into bed. I lay there and sleepily talked with her as she finished the wine. Then she went to brush her teeth and get ready for bed.

When she came back she wasn't wearing her tank top and shorts, but pale blue lingerie. She got into bed with me and put her arms around me. We kissed. This time she let me kiss her mouth, gave me her tongue. As I pulled off her slip she laughed and said, "I only just put that on." I fingered her ass as I licked her cunt, pushing my tongue into her.

This time it was good. She'd obviously planned it in advance, because she had some condoms under her pillow. We didn't use them right away. She took my cock in her mouth and sucked me, moving her mouth away just as I came. Later, she put a condom on me and we fucked until exhaustion made us stop.

It was close to dawn. A rooster was crowing somewhere outside. "I thought this wasn't supposed to happen again," I said.

She kissed my stomach. "You shouldn't believe everything I say."

She seemed to enjoy it, but she never got close to coming, and she never seemed wildly turned on. I knew even at the time that it was a kind of parting gift.

☆   ☆   ☆

I only got about two hours' sleep. I had to get up at seven to make my flight. I was more tired than I'd ever been. I wanted nothing so much as to fall asleep again and stay there with her.

I got out of bed and went to the toilet. Then I went back to the main room and got dressed. Françoise woke and lay watching me sleepily, not saying anything.

"I have to run," I said. She nodded. I put on my jacket and picked up my bag. Then I put the bag down, went over to the bed, bent and kissed her. "Be careful," I said. "And write to me as soon as you arrive."

She nodded again, but still didn't say anything. I took my bag and left. I walked into the village and waited for my bus.

SEVEN

New York was good. The work was easy, and I met up with a lot of friends who lived there. Milt was in California working on his film, so I didn't see him. I missed Françoise, and I wished she had a phone so I could call her before she left.

When I got home there was an airmail letter in my mailbox. She'd written it the day after she'd arrived in Rotterdam. I lost the letter long ago, but I remember that she was staying at Lotte's place until she found somewhere of her own, and that Lotte had a serious illness—cancer, I think. Françoise was about to start looking for work, modeling or waitressing.

She moved to Amsterdam a few months later, and wrote to me a few times from there. Then she sent me postcards from Spain and Scotland. After that, I never heard from her again. I tried writing to Lotte, to see if she knew where Françoise was. The letter came back with a sticker saying that no one of that name lived at that address. It could be that Lotte had just moved, but I think she'd died.

And so has Françoise. I was in New York a few weeks ago and ran into Tom Vince Quinn. He'd been in Holland recently and had met a painter who happened to know Françoise. The guy told him the news.

"I cannot for my soul remember how, or even precisely where, I first became acquainted with the Lady Ligeia. Long years have since elapsed, and my memory is feeble through much suffering. Or, perhaps, I cannot now bring these points to mind, because, in truth, the character of my beloved, her rare learning, her singular yet placid cast of beauty, and the thrilling and enthralling eloquence of her low musical language, made their way into my heart by paces so steadily and stealthily progressive, that they have been unnoticed and unknown."

Edgar Allan Poe wrote that. He's trying to summon the realness of a person he's loved, but he can't do it. All he can find is romantic sentences full of desperate adjectives. He can't find her. "She came and departed as a shadow." In the story, she comes back. In reality, Poe's wife, Virginia, who was thirteen when they married, died of consumption at twenty-four. She didn't come back, and Françoise isn't coming back either. Françoise is *no longer with us*. She has *passed on. Departed. Left. Gone away. Kicked the bucket. Bought the farm. Deceased.*

None of these even approximates how it is. Françoise hasn't "gone" somewhere, like when she went back to Holland. She was in Holland. I could say, "Françoise is in Holland."

Now she isn't anywhere. Now she isn't. And there's no trace of who she was. She doesn't live on in memory. I thought she did. I thought she lived in my memory, and that my problem was of finding language that could convey her to you, share her with you, make you know her. But it's clear to me now that it's not really her I remember. I don't know her anymore. I don't have her in my memory. What I have is a set of images, details and dialogues onto which I project meaning. You may think, having read all this, that you know something of her, but you don't. She's nowhere in this text. This text contains only images, details and dialogues onto which you project your meaning. There is no Françoise in this text. There is no Françoise.

You probably think you've gained an impression of the person Françoise was, and the person I was and am, from this narrative. But that's not true either. You haven't seen representations of us as people, just repeated mannerisms and modes of behavior. What frightens me most is that I'm not sure how that differs from the essence of a person. I don't want to think that, like characters in fiction who seem real even though they're just words on a page, real people are only comprised of repeated mannerisms and behavior.

I've tried so hard to make Françoise real, not for you but for me. Not long ago I sat in my sunlit living room and looked at my cock. I looked at the white skin, the thick veins. The foreskin hanging loosely at the end. I pulled back the foreskin and looked at the slit in the head. The faint smell from it, the semen and piss that come out of it. I thought about how it was inside Françoise, how she had it in her mouth, how she sucked and tasted it. I thought about that, and about how she once walked me to the bus stop after I'd spent the night at her place. I got on the bus and sat with my shoulder leaning against the window. Françoise, outside, tapped on the glass and, when I looked, she leaned against the window, her shoulder to mine, with only the glass separating us. I pressed my face to the glass, flattening my nose. She did the same, her breath smudging the glass, leaving a mark that remained for a few seconds, then evaporated, after she'd moved her face away. And how the toilet in her cottage had the acoustics of an echo chamber, so I could sit in the main room and listen to the tinkle of her piss or the irregular splashing of her shit hitting the water. I thought about all of that, and none of it did any good. I didn't know whether I'd lost something, or whether I'd just realized that I never had it.

As much truth as I can find is in this story, and that may not be much truth at all. If you've wondered why I haven't named the town where all this happened, it's because there's no such town. It didn't all happen in one place. Some of it didn't even happen in America. Some of it didn't happen at all. What I've told you isn't really about Françoise, who she was, but about me, who I am, whoever that is. It's hard for me now to separate the real from the imaginary, and if you think that's bullshit then you don't understand anything. Remember what I said about how I watched my mother begging in the street? That never actually happened. I read it in a novel. But it defined my mother's poverty better than any one real incident. The only reality I can't argue with, can't alter, is the reality that Tom's news brought to me.

Or maybe I can. Isn't that what I've been doing by telling this story? Since she was real for me during the four years since her last postcard, the reality wasn't dependent on her being alive, because she was still real in my mind after she was dead. She'd been dead for at least five months before I knew about it. Is that how little a life matters? That if I say that Françoise is working in a cafe somewhere this afternoon, and that this evening she'll be sitting in her lamplit living room, drinking red wine and playing her guitar—the one I gave her—before sleeping in her warm, fragrant bed, then the fact that she's dead doesn't diminish that reality? Maybe this story is the only thing now that gives her any reality at all.

EIGHT

About a week ago I had a magazine assignment that meant I had to go to another city. The woman I live with drove me to the airport. We didn't say much. Things hadn't been good between us for a while, and since I'd heard about Françoise I'd given up, done nothing except tell myself stories. As I got out of the car she said she'd pick me up the following morning.

I'd finished work by the late afternoon. I didn't feel like hanging out with the people who'd been at the press conference, so I just went to my hotel. But there was nothing to do there. I didn't want to watch TV, and reading seemed slightly ridiculous. I went out and walked around.

I passed by a couple of movie theaters, but I wasn't interested in what they were showing. I thought about going into a cafe or bar, but I didn't. It was a warm evening and it felt good to walk. There was a lot of activity on the streets, but somehow I didn't feel any sense of threat. When street people talked to me, I just smiled and kept walking.

As it began to get dark it got colder. I considered whether to choose a bar or head back to the hotel. Then I saw a theater that was showing a Charlie Chaplin double bill. I wasn't really in the mood for it, but I decided I was more in the mood for that than for anything else. I checked the time, and saw that the show started in ten minutes.

I bought a ticket and went in. There were only three other people there, an elderly couple and a man on his own. One other person arrived a few minutes into the first film.

As I watched Chaplin sitting on the snow and cuddling the dog, I thought I was going to cry. I tried to, hoping that it would help me, but it didn't come. I just stayed on the verge. I thought about the film and about Françoise and tried to feel just a little bit more.

A while later, I needed to piss. Without knowing why, I wanted to do it there in the theater. And I did. I unzipped, sat on the edge of my seat and pissed on the floor. It made plenty of noise and I was sure that the other people would hear, but they didn't. It ran in a stream under the seats, but no one was sitting in its path and no one seemed to notice. I zipped my jeans, stood up and walked out.

I walked back to my hotel. I had a drink in the bar, then went to the toilet to shit. I don't normally sit down in public toilets, but I was constipated and expected it to take a while. I took off my jacket, hung it on a peg on the door, unfastened my jeans and sat down. As I was squeezing it out, I noticed an envelope lying on the floor. I picked it up and looked at it. I opened it and read the letter inside. It was from a young woman to a guy who seemed to be her boyfriend. His name was David Hall. Her name was Shelley. She was at college in California, and she wrote about her course, her friends and social life, financial worries, an annoying phone call she'd had from her mother. She told David Hall that she missed him, and signed it *"with all my love."*

I wished the letter had been written to me. I tried to imagine what Shelley looked like, and what she was doing at that moment. When I'd finished emptying my bowels I put the letter in my shirt pocket and, deciding not to have another drink in the bar, went to my room.

I was lying in bed reading the letter again when there was a knock on the door. "Yeah, come in."

It was one of the hotel staff. He was holding my jacket. "Sir, you left this in the rest room. Somebody handed it in to reception. Lucky you had ID in your wallet."

"Jesus. I can't believe I did that. Okay, thanks."

"Where should I put it?"

"Just leave it on the chair."

He did. Then he just stood and looked at me. I waited for him to say something but he didn't. I had a rush of guilty paranoia, a feeling that he knew I had someone else's letter, that I was reading details of a life that wasn't mine and that I had no right to know about.

"Is there anything else?" I finally asked him.

"No, sir. Goodnight."

When he'd gone, I got up and locked the door.

Shelley. Françoise. Details of a life.

I flew home the next morning. She was waiting to pick me up, as she'd said she would be. She seemed both happy and angry. We drove to our apartment. On the way she told me about the night before. She'd fucked someone she worked with. They'd done it on the floor of our living room. He had a pierced tongue, and she liked the feel of it in her mouth and in her cunt. She showed me the bite mark he'd left on her neck. His cock was so big that she could only fit the head of it in her mouth. He tried to count her orgasms. At one point, after she came, he asked her, "How many is that?"

For a few days I had no work that needed to be done, which was fortunate because I could have done nothing. I couldn't settle in my apartment, but the city where I now live isn't safe to walk around in, and I didn't have enough focus to drive.

I wasn't thinking much about Françoise, or about what had just happened. I was thinking about a woman I was very close to about two years ago. We slept together a few times, but we weren't a couple. Then she left town, saying that she had to figure out her life. She gave me her mother's address and phone number and said that I could always reach her there. I wrote to her a few times but she never replied. I decided not to keep writing letters into a void. I thought maybe I was a part of her life when she was very unhappy, and that she didn't want to know me anymore.

Yesterday I phoned her mother. She was friendly, and told me that Alexa was living in Madeira, Portugal, working as a dance teacher. She gave me her number. I called, and Alexa picked it up. It was late at night at her end and she'd been asleep, but she was so thrilled to hear from me that she let out a scream.

She told me that since she last saw me she'd had a breakdown, which was why she hadn't written to me. She'd been on a self-hate trip and felt that she'd burdened me enough. Now she was living with a guy she loved, and she was happy. We talked for quite a while. I talked to him too. She'd told him about me. His English wasn't great and we had trouble with each other's accents, but he seemed nice. I gave Alexa my address and number and we said we'd keep in touch.

This morning I went to a cafe for breakfast. The waitress told me that her ex-husband had taken their daughter to another city and she was afraid she'd hardly ever see her. "But what the hell," she said. "It could be worse, right?" She looked out of the window. "It's a beautiful day." And it was. It really was.

February 1996
Phoenix, Arizona

STORIES 1987 – 1992

101 GET OUT AS EARLY AS YOU CAN

GET OUT AS EARLY AS YOU CAN

ONE

I was only eleven. It was the day before Lynn was nine.

Me and Mum and Lynn all came back from the off-sales that night. We were soaking. Mum had her old umbrella with her, but she didn't open it. Me and Lynn had sweets and chocolate and stuff, and a bottle of lemonade. And Mum's stuff.

Mum went into the living room first, to make sure Dad wasn't back yet. He wasn't. It was a big, filthy room. It had a bed-couch that me and Lynn slept on and a mattress on the floor that Mum and Dad slept on. There were two scabby armchairs and a black-and-white telly. There was a broken lamp with the shade bashed in. Mum's Barry Manilow poster was on the wall with one corner torn off, and on the floor underneath it was an electric fire. There were old newspapers and cans and bottles and smashed ornaments all over the floor, and a hole in the door where the iron had hit it.

Mum sat down on the arm of one of the chairs. She was really fat. "Let's have it," she said to us.

I had the cans of Carlsberg inside my jacket. I put my sweets and stuff down on the couch. "Where's Grandad?" I said.

"Must still be lying down," said Mum. "Hurry up!"

Me and Lynn opened our jackets and gave her the Carlsberg. "Where's the Voddy?" she asked Lynn.

Lynn laughed. She'd a lovely giggly laugh. She was blonde-haired and small. "Wait a minute," she said. She took her jacket off, then reached her hand up her skirt and brought out a quarter-bottle of vodka. She gave it to Mum.

"Thanks, love."

"Is Dad bringing the record player tonight?" I asked.

"He said he was," said Lynn.

"He is," said Mum. She opened the vodka and took a drink. "And he's getting a Barry Manilow record for me." She stood up. "I'm going for a lie-down. You better not forget—don't tell your Dad." We never did.

When she went out, me and Lynn sat on the couch and started eating the sweets.

"Daddy'll know," said Lynn. I ate my Dairy Milk and didn't say anything. "He'll be angry."

"Don't care," I said.

"He might leather us. We should tell."

"Then Mum would leather us and we wouldn't get any more sweeties," I said.

"Daddy'll know when he sees the sweeties."

"He'll know anyway," I said. "He always knows. The sweeties'll be finished when he gets home."

"He'll ask us if Mummy went to the off-sales."

"We'll say no."

"He won't believe us," she said. "He'll know we're telling lies."

"Don't care."

"We'll get leathered!"

"Don't care," I said, but I was just being big. I thought about it. "He never touched us last Saturday."

"He might this time," said Lynn.

We sat and ate the sweets and didn't say anything. I opened the bottle of lemonade and drank some, then gave it to Lynn and she took a drink. When she finished she looked at the bottle. "Remember she threw the bottle at him?"

"Yes," I said.

"Do you think they'll fight tonight?"

"Yes."

"But it's my birthday tomorrow," she said. I didn't say anything. "Hope they don't fight."

"They will," I said.

"I wish we didn't need to sleep in here. How come we've got to?"

"'Cause Grandad's in the other room," I said.

"There's two rooms." I didn't say anything.

"Mummy's lying down in the other one. Why can't we sleep in it?"

"It's not our room."

"Why can't Mummy and Daddy sleep in it, then? Why can't we see inside it?"

"I've seen inside it," I said.

Lynn looked at me. "When?"

"Yesterday."

She didn't believe me. "How? They'd've leathered you if you did."

"They didn't know. Dad and Grandad were out, and you and Mum were in Aunties Mae's. I got home from school and there was nobody in. So I looked."

"We got home from Auntie Mae's before you got home from school! You're telling lies!"

"I am not." I went in the huff and didn't say anything, but neither did she. So I said, "After I looked, I went to Peter's and played monopoly. If I'd stayed, they'd've known I looked. They'd've leathered me even if I said I didn't. And don't you tell them!"

"I won't."

"Good."

"What's in there?" Lynn asked.

I didn't want to tell her. "Nothing."

"Do you know why we can't sleep in there?"

"Yes."

"Why?"

"Never mind," I said.

"You never looked."

"I did."

"What's in there, then?"

"Never mind."

"Tell me!" She was getting angry.

I didn't want to tell her, so I got angry too. "If you want to know, why don't you go and look now? Mum's in there...lying down. Go and ask her if you can see!"

She looked at me. She could be rotten sometimes. "If you don't tell me, I'll tell Daddy you looked."

"I'll say I never."

"He'll believe me."

"He won't," I said, but I knew he would.

"He'll leather you," said Lynn.

I got scared. "You cow!" Then I tried to be nice. "Don't tell him."

"Tell me, then."

I didn't say anything. Then I got an idea. "Dracula's in there!"

"Liar!" She was really scared of Dracula.

"He is. I saw him."

She looked scared. "There's no Dracula!"

I started enjoying myself. "How do you know?"

"Mummy told me. She said there's no Dracula and no Sammy Souplefoot."

"Last Saturday she told you there was a Sammy Souplefoot. Remember? She told you he'd come and get you."

"But she was having one of her bad turns."

"She still said it. She said Sammy Souplefoot was coming to get you!" I said in a horrible voice.

Lynn's voice was shaking. "She was only kidding."

"No, she wasn't. And she knows."

"How does she know?"

"'Cause she's a vampire as well."

"She's not." Lynn was nearly whispering.

"She is. She's in the room right now—"

"She's lying—lying down!"

"She's in there lying down with Dracula and Sammy Souplefoot!"

Lynn was terrified. "She's not!"

"She is. And so're Dracula and Sammy Souplefoot. They're in the room drinking Carlsberg and voddy, and then they're coming in here to suck your blood!"

"You're telling lies!"

"I'm not! They're going to get you."

"Mummy! I want Mummy!"

"No you don't. She's a vampire."

"She's not…she's she—" Lynn started to cry. She put her hands over her face and curled up on the couch. She was shaking and making gurgly noises.

I felt really bad. "Don't," I said, still trying to be big as well. "I was only kidding." She still kept crying. "I was only kidding. There's no Sammy Souplefoot. I was only kidding." I put my hand on her head and played with her hair. "Stop crying. It's okay." She didn't stop crying and it made me scared. "Don't Lynn, eh…don't cry. It's okay."

She took her hands away from her face and looked up at me. She couldn't talk right at first. She had to say a word, then cry, then say another word.

"Don't…frighten…me…any…more…it's…not…fair."

"Sorry," I said.

She sat up and looked at me. She was still crying a bit. "Did you really see Dracula?"

"No. I was kidding you."

"Don't scare me any more."

"I won't." I gave her a cuddle. She didn't say anything. "There's no such thing as vampires," I said.

"What about Sammy Souplefoot?" Her voice was really quiet.

"Mum just made him up to frighten us," I said.

"Why's she always want to frighten us?"

"Don't know," I said. "She's nuts. We're not scared of her, are we?"

"I'm scared of Sammy Souplefoot."

"There's no Sammy Souplefoot. She just made him up."

Lynn didn't say anything. Then she said, "Does Mummy think there is a Sammy Souplefoot?"

"Maybe," I said. "Don't think so. But we know there isn't. And Dracula's only on the telly. And he's daft. He always gets killed."

Lynn was still scared. "He frightens me anyway. I wish Mummy wouldn't make me watch the telly when he's on."

"She shouldn't," I said. It wasn't fair.

Then Grandad came in. He'd been lying down. He was wearing old trousers, a shirt and a jumper with holes in it. His hair was messed and he'd no shoes or socks on.

"Where's your mother?" he asked. He talked funny. He always tried to talk posh, like people on the telly, but he kept getting things wrong.

"Lying down," said Lynn.

"So was I. I was lying down all day." He went and sat in one of the chairs.

"Were you tired?" I said.

"No. Just practicing for when I'm dead. Best to get the hang of it now." He looked at Lynn. "Let's have a drop of your lemonade. I've drank nothing all day but a mug of cocoa." He said it coh-coh-aa.

Lynn gave him the bottle. "There's not much left. Leave me some."

"Be glad you got any. When I was your age, I had to drink water with a licorice stick dipped in it." He was always saying things like that.

"I don't like licorice," said Lynn.

"I do," I said.

Grandad drank most of the lemonade and gave the bottle back to Lynn. "I never had likes or dislikes. I was glad of what I could get. Do you know what I had for my tea when I was your age?"

"Yes," I said.

"The top off my father's boiled egg."

"We haven't had our tea," said Lynn.

"We have so!" I said.

Grandad didn't bother. "When I was out playing, my mother'd shout from the window, 'Your tea's ready! We're having cold chicken.' I knew she meant bread and margarine." He said it *margarein.* "But I was glad of it."

Me and Lynn didn't bother. He'd told us that loads of times. We ate the sweets we had left.

Lynn picked up the lemonade bottle. "D'you want some? You've had hardly any."

I looked at it. There was almost none left. "No. You drink it."

"Thanks." She took the cork off and started to drink it.

"That's most unhygenisic, you know," said Grandad.

"What?" Lynn said.

"Drinking from a bottle out of what somebody else has just drank," he said.

Lynn didn't get it. "Oh."

"But you just did," I said to him.

"Incorrect. I wiped the bottle on my cardigan before I drank from it." I knew he hadn't. "And don't take that succulent attitude towards your elders. You don't do as I do, you do as I tell you. That's what we were told in the army."

"Why shouldn't you drink out of the bottle after somebody else?" asked Lynn. She always wanted to know things.

"Because saliva contains bacteriums."

"What?" said Lynn.

"Bacteriums," he said.

"What's that?" said Lynn.

"Germs," I said.

"Correct," said Grandad. "And they're in everybody's saliva."

"Everybody's saliva?" said Lynn.

"That's what I said."

"So I've got them too?"

"Correct."

"So if we've all got them already, why can't we drink from somebody else's bottle?" she asked.

"Because all our bacteriums are different. We've all got individual bacteriums. And everybody's individual bacteriums are poisonous to everybody else."

"What about kissing?" I said.

"What?" he said.

"What about kissing?" I said.

"What *about* kissing?"

"Why don't people poison each other when they kiss?"

Lynn laughed. "Have you kissed somebody?"

"Shut your face," I said to her. "Why don't people get other people's germs when they kiss?" I asked Grandad.

"Kissing's different," he said.

"How is it?" I said.

"When one kisses another, the germs are destroyed by the affection between the two."

"What if people don't like each other?" I said.

"If they didn't like each other they wouldn't kiss."

"I don't like Auntie Mae," I said.

"So?"

"I kiss her. Mum makes me. How come I don't poison her?"

He didn't say anything, then he said, "Because she likes you." He saw Lynn looking at the bottle in her hand. "Go ahead, Lynn. Poison yourself if you like." She did.

I said, "Me and Peter always drink out of the same bottle and we don't get poisoned."

"You will," he said. "It takes time. The procedure is progressive. The germs and bacteriums break down one's bodily resources gradually."

I knew he was talking rubbish. "How long does it take?"

"Years. It depends on how uncivilized one is."

"What?"

"Your pal Peter's family have a physical resistance to it because of their background. Working-class proletarians like them lack the social graces, so they're indulgent in rude-man-nered activities like sharing unsterilized bottles all the time. So they build up a resistance to germs and bacteriums. But middle-class people like us have better manners. We don't take part in unhygenisic practices. So we're not used to germs and bacteri-ums. So we get poisoned easier."

Then Lynn said, "What's in the spare room, Grandad?"

He looked at her. "Have you been in there?"

"No, she hasn't," I said. "She's just curious."

Grandad looked relieved she hadn't been in. I knew why. "That's the guest room," he said. "It's for guests. Only guests get to go in there."

"We don't have any guests," I said.

"If we do, they'll get to go in there."

Lynn said, "Mummy gets to go in there. She's not a guest."

"Your mother has the job of tidying the guest room."

"She's not tidying it," said Lynn. "She's lying down."

"Well, she tidies the rest of the house." The house had never been tidied in my life. "Isn't she entitled to lie down in the guest room sometimes?" said Grandad.

Lynn wasn't sure. "Uh-huh."

"But nobody else can go in there," said Grandad. So don't you two."

"I don't want to," I said.

"Good. Because you can't."

"Why?" said Lynn. "What's in there?"

"Nothing. Just furniture."

I said, "I'd like to see it too." Lynn looked at me funny, but she didn't say anything.

"You just can't," said Grandad. "It's the Guest Room and you're not guests. So the Guest Room's none of your business."

TWO

Then Dad came home. He was big and quite fat, but not as fat as Mum. He was a butcher. He worked a half-day on Saturdays. He hadn't shaved and he smelled. He came in carrying an old record player and a Barry Manilow LP.

"Is that the record player, Daddy?" said Lynn.

I said, "No. It's a fridge."

Dad said to me, "Don't be fucking smart, right, Kevin." Then he said to Lynn, "Of course it's the record player. I told you I'd get it tonight. And your Uncle Tommy gave me the record for your Mum."

"Mummy said you would," said Lynn.

"Where is she?" said Dad.

I said, "Lying down in the...Guest Room." Lynn giggled when I said that.

Grandad said, "I never laughed at my elders. Did you get a paper, Robert?"

Dad shook his head and sat in the chair across from Grandad's. "Did your Mum go out tonight, Lynn? he asked.

"Uh-huh," said Lynn.

"Did you go with her?"

"Uh-huh. Me and Kevin went."

"Did she go to the off-sales?"

"No," I said.

"No," said Lynn.

Dad said to Lynn, "Are you telling lies?"

"No, she's not!" I said.

"No," said Lynn.

"You better not be. I'll know. And you'll get leathered."

Lynn got scared. "We're not telling lies."

"Did she get you sweeties?" Dad asked her.

"Uh-huh," she said.

"Where did she get them from?"

"The supermarket," I said.

"Have you two had your tea?" he asked Lynn.

"Yes," I said.

He didn't bother with me. "Have you had your tea?" he asked Lynn.

Lynn didn't say anything. Then she said, "Uh-huh."

"What'd you have?"

"Chips and egg," I said.

"Shut your fucking mouth," he said to me. "I wasn't asking you. What'd you have for your tea, Lynn?"

Lynn said "Chips and egg."

"I don't believe you."

"It's true," I said.

"Shut up!" he screamed at me. He always screamed at me. He said to Lynn, "Tell the truth—did your Mum give you chips and fucking egg for your tea?"

Lynn's voice went quiet. "Uh-huh."

"Don't fucking whisper! Answer me properly!"

"Yes," she said.

"See!" I shouted. "Now will you fucking leave her alone!"

"Don't fucking swear, you cheeky bastard!" he shouted back.

Grandad said, "The saddest sound in creation is the sound of one swearing at one's offspring."

Dad said, "You shut your face as well. The kids could never get fed and you wouldn't bother your fat arse." He said to me and Lynn, "Look. I know you've not had any tea. And I know your Mum went to the off-sales. I know she'll be drunk when she comes out of the room. I know you're telling lies. And you don't have to. It's daft. If you tell me you haven't had any tea, I'll make you some. But I won't if you don't tell me. If you say you've been fed then I'm not going to feed you."

"We *have* been fed," I said.

Grandad said, "When I got up they had sweets and lemonade."

"But they haven't had their tea," said Dad.

"We *have*," said Lynn.

"If they live on sweets they'll end up in hospital," said Dad.

"We've had our tea," I said.

"You haven't. And if you're not going to admit it, you can starve."

Nobody said anything for awhile, then Grandad said to Dad, "Did you notice the graffiti on the wall at the end of the close?"

"No. Why?"

"It says *Mary Kirkhill's an alky.*"

Dad wasn't bothered. "Mmm. Wonder how they found out. I suppose it's general knowledge by this time."

"I don't like people calling my daughter an alky." said Grandad.

"D'you mind your daughter being an *alky?*" said Dad.

"She's not. She just drinks too much."

Nobody said anything for ages after that. Then Dad got up and plugged in the record player. "Your Uncle Tommy wasn't sure this would work," he said.

Lynn said, "Put the record on and see."

"Thanks, Lynn. I'd never've thought of that." He put the record on, but the thing didn't turn. "Looks like your Uncle Tommy was right."

"Mummy'll go mad," said Lynn. "She was looking forward to it."

"So were we," I said. Grandad didn't say anything. He didn't care.

Dad said, "Well, there's fuck all I can do about it. I told her it might not work."

"She'll still go crazy," said Lynn.

"She'll just have to, then." He pulled the plug out. "I don't like Barry Manilow, anyway."

"Mummy does," said Lynn.

Grandad said, "That stuff isn't music. In my day, those persons wouldn't have lasted five minutes on a stage. Our crooners never needed microphones. You could hear them anywhere in the theater. They don't sing nowadays, they shout. They've no—"

"For fuck's sake shut up!" said Dad. He went and sat in his chair again. "That Al Jolson sounds like a knife scraping across a plate."

"Al Jolson! *That's* music," said Grandad.

"It's Lynn's birthday tomorrow," I said.

"Believe it or not, I know that," said Dad. "I actually had something to do with her birth."

Lynn giggled. "What about Kevin's birth?" I wished she hadn't said that.

"Kevin wasn't born. Your Mum coughed him up one night when she was being sick."

"How come Kevin never gets any birthday presents?" said Lynn.

"Shut up," I said.

"He never deserves any," said Dad.

"I never want any," I said.

Then Grandad had to get in. "I never expected any presents when I was a child. All I got on my birthday was an orange and a sherbert dip."

Lynn said, "What am I getting, Daddy?"

"Wait and see."

I was fed up. "What's on the telly?" I said. "Is Dracula on tonight?"

"It's on later," said Dad.

"I don't want to watch Dracula," said Lynn.

"It's not on for a while yet," said Dad.

"Can we put the telly on now?" I said

"If you want." Dad got up from his chair and turned on the telly. It was black and white. We'd had it for ages.

We watched it for a while. The program was rubbish. "This is boring," I said.

"I don't make the programs," Dad said.

"In my day, we created our own entertainment," said

Grandad. "We never had—"
 "*Never had what?*"
 Mum had come in.

THREE

She was scary. She was always scary when she was drunk. She was fat and her face was really white and her eyes were messed with make-up. She looked rubbery. "Did you get the record player?" she said to Dad in her drunk voice.

 "I got it." He wasn't looking at her.

 "But it's not working," I said. I was glad it wasn't working.

 "*Did you get the Barry Manilow record?*"

 "I got it, but the record player's not working," said Dad. He was looking at the telly, not at Mum. So was Grandad. Lynn was looking at me.

 "Where is it?" said Mum.

 "On top of the record player," I said.

 She went and picked up the record and looked at the picture on the cover. "He's lovely." She said to Grandad, "Put the telly off."

 Dad looked at her. "What for?"

 Grandad kept looking at the telly. "Why? You can't play the record. The machine is dysfunctional."

 "*Put the fucking telly off!*"

 "What for?" said Dad. He sounded tired.

 "I was watching it," I said.

 "Me too," said Lynn, because I'd said it.

 Mum started screaming. "*Put the fucking telly off! Put it off!*" She ran at the telly as if she was going to attack it. She switched it off. Then she stood in front of it, looking at everybody. "*It's off for the night!*" she screamed. "*It's off! Right? It's off for the night.*"

 Grandad said, "One fails to comprehend the rationale—"

 "Shut up," Dad said to him.

"That's it off for the NIGHT! For the fucking NIGHT!"

"Shut up," said Dad.

"What?" said Mum.

"Shut up. Shut your dirty, poxy, alcoholic mouth."

"What do you mean, alcoholic?"

"Fuck off and sober up."

"You bastard! I'm not drunk!"

"You are fucking drunk," said Dad. He said it as if he was just tired and not angry, but I knew he was.

"I am not!" shouted Mum.

Grandad said, "Although not in a state of total inebriation, I would imagine you'd been drinking."

"I beg your fucking *pardon!* I have not been drinking. Ask the kids. They were with me."

"I asked them," said Dad. "They're a pair of lying little cunts."

"We told the truth," I said.

"Shut up," he said to me. "When I want you, I'll throw you a bone."

Grandad got angry. "I refuse to sit here and let my grand-children be subjected to such abuse."

"What're you going to do?" Dad asked him.

"Go to bed." He stood up. "Fight with as low a volume level as possible, if you please." He went out.

Dad asked Mum if me and Lynn'd been fed. "Of course they've been fed," she said.

"I know they've had their faces stuffed with sweets, but have they had their tea?"

"Of course they've had their tea! What kind of a mother do you think I am?"

"What'd they have?"

"Chips and gammon."

"That's funny," he said. "They think they had chips and egg."

"We did have chips and egg!" I said.

"That's right," said Lynn.

"Oh…I thought I gave you gammon," she said. "It must've been egg, then."

"I can usually tell the difference between gammon and egg," said Dad. "And so can you. And so can that lying cunt there." He meant me. "They've had no tea."

"They fucking have! Ask Lynn. She's not a liar."

"No, but she'll agree with anything he says."

"They've had their tea, you bastard!"

"I'm only half a bastard," said Dad. "They were engaged."

"Cheeky bastard! Your Dad'd never have a love child! They were married! You're legitimate, you bastard."

Lynn said, "Mummy."

"What?"

"Don't fight any more."

"What?" She looked at Lynn like she was going to eat her.

"Don't fight any more. You said you wouldn't."

"I'm not fighting."

I said, "Well, don't shout or she'll think you are."

"I'm not fucking shouting!" Mum shouted.

"Christ almighty," said Dad. He got up and switched on the telly, then sat down and started watching it.

"I said that telly was off for the night!" Mum went over and switched it off again. "It's off for the night. If I don't hear my record, no cunt sees the telly."

"The record player doesn't work," I said.

"You shut up," Dad said to me.

Mum said, "The record player doesn't work, the fucking telly doesn't work."

Lynn started to cry. I shouted at them. "Will you fucking stop it! Please? You promised Lynn you wouldn't fight."

"Watch your language," said Mum.

"*Please!* It's her birthday tomorrow."

"I know it's her birthday tomorrow! What kind of mother d'you fucking well think I am?"

"Come on, stop crying," I said to Lynn. "They're not going to fight anymore."

"I wasn't fighting in the first place," said Dad.

"Neither was I. You started it!" shouted Mum.

"Don't!" I shouted.

"How did I start it, you drunken cow?" said Dad.

Lynn's crying got worse.

"The same as you always fucking start it! Everything was fine till you arrived. I just tidied up the house—"

"The house is filthy," said Dad.

"Then I went to the shops with the kids. Everything was fine. I went for a lie-down when I got back, then I get up, you're here, and that's it! I don't get to hear my record, I don't even get to watch the telly in peace!"

"I'll put it on," I said.

"Touch it and I'll cut your fingers off," said Mum. "If I can't hear my record, the telly's off for the night."

Dad was spitting as he spoke. "'Tidied the house!' Whereabouts did you fucking tidy? The spare room?"

"What's in that room?" Lynn sobbed. "Can I sleep there tonight?"

"No, you can't," said Mum. "Sammy Souplefoot's in there."

Lynn was nearly screaming. Her face was red and her mouth was white. *You said there was no Sammy Souplefoot!*

"In that room there is. He can't come out, but if you ever go in there he'll get you. He'll make you a vampire like him." She made a horrible face and started to sing. *"Sammy-Souplefoot's-going-to-get-you, Sammy-Souplefoot's-going-to-get-you..."*

Lynn screamed and hid her face in the couch cushions. Dad just sat there and didn't do anything.

"Leave her alone!" I shouted. "Leave her alone or I'll tell everybody what's really in that room!"

Mum stopped. She gave me a horrible look. Lynn kept crying. "You don't know what's in that room," said Mum. "Sammy Souplefoot's in that room."

"Shut up or I'll tell *everybody* about that room," I said.

Dad got up from his chair. "Have you been in there?"

"No, he hasn't been in there!" said Mum. "He knows Sammy Souplefoot'd get him."

"I have been in there! There's no Sammy Souplefoot! It's full of bags. Bags of rubbish! *Hundreds* of them!"

Dad slapped me, but it didn't hurt. "You bastard! I told you to stay out of there! D'you want fucking leathered?"

"I don't care! But if she doesn't leave Lynn alone, I'm going to tell everybody."

"Who're you calling 'she'?" Mum said. " 'She's' got a fucking name!"

'Shut up you fucking alky," said Dad. "If he says anything, the sanitary inspectors'll have your kids off you. Including your bastard!"

"He's yours as well!"

"Is he fuck. Lynn's mine."

"So's Kevin!" Mum shouted.

"Is he fuck!"

"He is!"

"Shut up!" I shouted. "I don't care!"

They both ignored me. Mum said, "You and Mae'll soon be producing a few bastards as well."

He looked at her. "What're you on about? What's Mae got to do with it?"

"When we were out with her on Monday!"

"What about it?"

"Your hand was up her skirt."

He laughed at her. "In your dreams, maybe. For a start, Tommy was there—I'm sure he'd just sit there and let me feel up his wife. Anyway, your sister's as fucking ugly as you. I'm fucking fed up, not hard up."

"I'm not hard up, either, mastermind! There's plenty of—"

"I know," he said. "You'd drop your drawers for a drop of wine." He pointed at me. "That's where *that* came from."

"I don't care!" I shouted. "Just stop fighting! It's Lynn's birthday tomorrow."

"I know it's her birthday tomorrow! Mum shouted back. "What kind of mother do you th—"

"If you don't stop fighting, I'll tell everybody what's in the room!" I said.

Lynn shouted "Mummy!" Her face was still hid in a cushion.

"The bastard's not going to threaten me," Mum said to Dad. "I'm going to clean that room out right now."

"Don't be so fucking stupid," said Dad. "It'd take weeks." Mum went out. "Mary *Kirkhill!* For fuck's *sake!*" Dad went out after her.

FOUR

I just put my arm around Lynn and kept it like that till she stopped crying. We didn't say anything till she stopped crying, then she said, "What's really in that room?"

I didn't want to tell her. Then I did. "Like I said to them. Bags of rubbish."

"What rubbish?"

"I don't know. When I went into the room, I could hardly get the door opened. When I got in, there were hundreds of bin-bags full of rubbish."

"Really hundreds?" she said.

"Honest. They were piled right up to the ceiling. Everywhere!"

She didn't believe me. "Are you telling lies? Are you kidding me on?"

"No. Honest."

"But why do they keep rubbish in there? What do they want it for?"

"I don't know."

"Why's it not smelly?"

"The plastic bags keep the smell in, that's why," I said. "I opened some to look in, and they were *really* smelly."

"Mummy never takes the bin down to the midden."

"She never does anything," I said.

"Daddy never takes it down either. It just disappears!"

"Now you know where it disappears to."

"But it's *daft!*" she said. "Why do they keep it in the room? Why don't they just take it down to the midden?"

"I don't know. They're nuts."

We could hear Mum and Dad shouting at each other in the Guest Room.

"I wish they wouldn't fight anymore," said Lynn. I didn't say anything. "I wish Mummy wouldn't have bad turns any more."

"Drunk turns, more like," I said.

"Sometimes she gets them when she's not drunk," said Lynn.

"She doesn't."

"She does."

I felt scared. "When?" She didn't say anything. "When?" I said.

"Remember when I burned my foot in the chip pan?"

"Yes." I said.

"I didn't. It was Mummy."

I felt funny in my head and stomach. "What do you mean? How?"

Lynn said, "She heated up the chip pan, then put it down on the floor and stuck my foot in it."

"What for?" I sounded funny.

"She was having a bad turn," said Lynn.

"Does Dad know?"

"Uh-huh. I wasn't to tell anybody. Don't tell I told you."

"I won't." We didn't say anything, then I said, "Does she have lots of bad turns when she's not drunk?" *I thought I was protecting you.*

"Hardly ever. And she just acts funny when she does."

"Is that the only time she's hurt you?" I said. Her foot had been bandaged for ages.

"Uh-huh."

"Honest?"

"Yes."

"You'd better not tell anybody about the bags of rubbish," I said.

"All right."

"If anybody finds out, they'll take us away and put us in a home."

Lynn didn't say anything. Then she said, "I don't want to get put in a home. But I'd like to live somewhere else."

"Where?"

"Don't know," she said. "I wish Mummy and Daddy wouldn't fight. It's my birthday tomorrow."

"I know."

"I'll be nine."

"I know."

"D'you think I'll get a present?"

"Don't know," I said, but I did know. "Maybe."

"How come you never get a present?" she said.

"I never want any."

"You do so," she said.

"Never mind."

"Do you think they'll fight tomorrow?" she said.

"I think they'll always fight."

"Why do they fight?"

"They're crazy. They're mental."

"I'd like to live somewhere else," she said.

I stood up and went to the toilet. In the hall, I could hear Mum and Dad screaming at each other in the Guest Room. I went to the toilet. It was just a toilet, with no bath. I rolled up my sleeve and clawed my arm till it bled. It hurt but I felt better.

When it stopped bleeding, I went back to the living room. I could hear Mum and Dad were in there now. When I went in,

Mum was standing holding one of the bin-bags from the Guest Room, and her and Dad were shouting at each other. Lynn was sitting on the couch, scared.

"Cunt! Bastard!" mum screamed. "It's your fucking rubbish as well as mine!"

"Is it fuck!" said Dad. "It's your rubbish—" he pointed at me"—same as it's your bastard."

Lynn said, "Mummy, don't…it's my birthday tomorrow…"

Mum giggled, just like Lynn did sometimes. "Fuck your birthday." She opened the bin-bag and emptied it all over Lynn.

The stuff was really rotten. A lot of it was old food and stuff. Lynn just sat there on the couch and it was all over her. Then she said, with the stuff all over her face, "I'll be nine…"

"Christ's sake," said Dad. But he just stood there.

I went mental. "You *cow!* You fucking *cow!* She'll be nine!" I went for Mum and started punching her and kicking her. "You *cow!* Cow! You *cow!*" But I'm really skinny and she's so big and fat that I couldn't hurt her. She grabbed me by the hair and threw me down on the couch. I started crying and tried to get up and she grabbed my hair again and pulled my head down and kicked me in the face.

Dad said, "Christ's sake!" again and pulled her off me and shoved her into a chair. "For *Christ's* sake!"

I put my hands over my mouth and nose to try to keep the blood in, but it came out anyway. I took my hands away, and it came pouring out of my nose. Lynn was just sitting there, covered in rubbish. I went and cuddled her and my blood got on her and the rubbish got on me. I was still crying. I was crying so hard the two of us were shaking from it.

Lynn said, "I'll be nine." She pulled away a bit and looked at my face. "Your nose is bleeding."

I couldn't talk for crying and anyway the blood was in my mouth and throat. Mum was trying to get up from the chair and Dad kept pushing her back down.

Lynn said, "Daddy…"

"Shut up," said Dad.

"Kevin's nose is bleeding," said Lynn.

"I want to hear Barry Manilow!" screamed Mum.

Lynn said, "Daddy."

"Shut up!" Dad shouted at her.

Then Grandad came in. He had a tatty dressing gown on. He looked at everything, my blood and the rubbish, and didn't bother. He wasn't surprised, just angry. "Might I ask that the noise be kept down to a mere crescendo?" he said.

"Put the fucking record on!" said Mum.

"Kevin's nose is bleeding, Grandad," Lynn said.

Dad said, "Good. Maybe he'll bleed to death."

Granada looked at me. "It's bleeding all right," he said.

Mum said, "I'm going to wet myself."

Dad slapped her face. "Fucking don't. What'd you think the toilet's for?" He pulled her out of the chair. "Come on. I'll help you."

They went out, with Mum saying something about Barry Manilow. Grandad sat down on the couch next to me and Lynn. He didn't say anything about the rubbish on Lynn.

"Let's have a look at your nose, Kevin," he said to me. He held my face in his hands and looked at me. "And stop that crying. You'll never make a soldier. When I was your age, I had a nosebleed every day."

I said, "It was that fucking—"

"Don't swear. Where d'you hear language like that?" He looked at Lynn. "Go to the bathroom and procure a towel."

"Mummy and Daddy are in there." she said.

"They're answering a call of nature. They don't need a towel. Go on."

She went, with bits of rubbish falling off of her.

"How's it feel?" Grandad said to me.

"It hurts. She kicked me."

"You're all right. You're not a girl, are you?" He squeezed my nose with his fingers.

"That's sore!" I tried to pull away but he wouldn't let me.

"I know it's sore. But you've got to be cruel to be kind." Lynn came in with a filthy towel. She just gave the towel to Grandad and went and sat in one of the chairs.

Grandad squeezed my nose with the towel. I went "Aagh!" but I didn't pull away this time. Grandad said, "Good boy. It'll be better soon. You see, you've got to be cruel to be kind. Remember that."

"Am I still bleeding?"

"A bit. Here, hold the towel yourself. It'll soon stop."

I was sitting holding the towel to my nose and nobody was saying anything when Dad came back in. He looked tired.

"Where's Mary?" said Grandad.

"In the Guest Room."

"What's she doing?"

"She's not doing anything. She passed out. I put her in there with the other dirt." He went over and stood in front of the couch where Grandad was sitting. "I've made up my mind. I'm putting in for a divorce."

"Might one enquire as to the nature of the event that brung this on?" said Grandad.

"I've just had as much as I want."

"Would Mae have anything to do with your decision, perchance?"

Dad looked at him and laughed a bit. "You as well? Fuck's sake. Who got that idea first, you or your daughter?"

"Mary suggested it to me," said Grandad.

"Well, you're as daft as she is. Like I told her, she's ugly enough and mental enough. The last thing I want's her ugly, mental sister. I just want to get away. Away from her, away from her bastard—"

"Don't call him that," said Grandad.

My nose wasn't bleeding any more. I took the towel away from it. "I don't care," I said.

"I'll call him what he is," Dad said to Grandad. "He's a

fucking bastard. He's probably Duncan Gray's bastard. He looks like him."

Grandad's voice went funny. "Well, even if he is, it's not his fault. He says Mary kicked him in the face."

"She did. Nobody's wrong all the time. Shame she didn't kill the cunt."

Grandad started to cry. I couldn't believe it. I said, "Grandad—"

"What's up with you?" Dad said to him. He sat there on the couch with tears running down his face. He didn't put his hands up to hide it like you're supposed to. He stopped talking posh, and talked like everybody else. I never heard him talk like that before.

"What d'you fucking *think?*" he said to Dad.

Seeing him crying and hearing him talking like that scared me. I said, "It's all right, Grandad."

He said to Dad, "Do you know what you're doing to those kids? What's fucking *wrong* with you, Robert?"

"It's your daughter there's something wrong with," said Dad.

"You're as bad! You're worse! She can't help it."

"I couldn't care less," said Dad.

Grandad's crying got worse. "I know."

"I just want away from the lot of you," said Dad.

"Those kids...What are you doing...It's not their fault..." You could hardly hear what Grandad was saying, his crying was so bad. Lynn just sat looking at him. I thought she was going to cry too, and then I would have.

"Stop whining, you old fucker," Dad said to him. "Go to bed or something." He headed for the door.

"Where're you going?" said Grandad.

"If it's any of your fucking business, I'm going for a walk."

Lynn said, "Are you coming back, Daddy?" She was curled right down in the chair and her voice was shaking.

"Of course I'm coming back," Dad shouted from the hall as he went out. "Where would I go?"

FIVE

"Grandad," I said.

"I'm all right," he sniffled. "I'm going to bed. It's time you two were in bed as well."

"I'll put Lynn to bed," I said.

"Good boy." He stood up. "Is your nose all right?" I nodded my head. "You'll make a soldier yet."

When he went to bed, me and Lynn didn't say anything. Then Lynn said, "Kevin."

"What?"

"Is Grandad really all right?"

"Yes," I said.

"He never cries."

"Men sometimes cry," I said.

"Daddy doesn't."

"Lets go to bed," I said.

I made up the bed. I folded the couch down and got the blankets and pillows from under it and made it up.

"Is Dracula on the telly yet?" said Lynn.

"No. It'll be on soon."

"Are you putting it on?"

"Not if you don't want me to," I said.

"I don't."

"Don't worry, then."

"What about Mummy?"

"She's a fucking nutter. What about her?"

"Don't swear," Lynn said.

"Okay."

"What about Mummy?"

"She's nuts. What about her?"

"What if she wants to watch Dracula?"

"She's asleep. She'll probably be out cold for the night," I said. "Come on, get to bed."

"Right," said Lynn. She took off her clothes, except her vest and pants, and got into bed.

"Where's Albert?" she said.

Albert was her teddy. I reached my hand under the bed and got him. "Here."

"Thanks." She cuddled him. "I don't feel all that scared of Sammy Souplefoot when I've got Albert."

"I told you there's no Sammy Souplefoot."

"Mummy said there was tonight."

"That's 'cause she's mental. She wanted to frighten you so's you'd stay out of that room."

"If there's no Sammy Souplefoot, why's she keep saying there is?"

"She's nuts. She wants to frighten you."

"I wish she wouldn't," said Lynn.

"She won't any more tonight," I said.

"Are you sure?"

"Yes."

"Do you love Mummy?"

"No."

"I do," she said.

I didn't say anything. Then I said, "D'you love Albert, too?"

She laughed and cuddled Albert. "Yes!"

"Good."

I took off my clothes except my vest and pants and got in the bed too.

"D'you think Daddy'll come back?" she said to me.

"Of course he'll come back."

"D'you think he'll really leave Mummy?"

"No," I said. "But he should."

"What'd happen to us?"

"Don't know. We might get put in a home."

"I don't want to."

"We won't have to," I said.

"I'd like to live somewhere else," she said.

"Where?"

"Somewhere in a park. Mummy and Daddy used to take us to the park."

"I know."

"I wish we could go to the park tomorrow. It's my birthday…"

"I know it is. You'll be nine million and nine."

She giggled. "D'you think we could go to the park tomorrow?"

"Don't know. Maybe. I'll take you, if they'll let me."

"I wish we could all go," she said. "Mummy didn't take bad turns in the park."

"She did once."

"She didn't!"

"She did."

"Did she?"

"Honest," I said.

"I can't remember it."

"I know, but I'm clever."

"What did she do?"

"Never mind," I said.

"Tell me!"

"I can't remember what she did."

"You can so. You're telling lies."

I was. "I can't. Honest."

She believed me. "Do you think we could all go to the park tomorrow?"

"I'll ask. If they say no, I'll ask if I can take you."

Then Mum came in.

She looked like something in a horror film on the telly. She was walking really slow. She came and sat down on the bed. She's so fat, the bed shook. She looked at us funny.

Lynn was scared. "Are you all right, Mummy?"

"I want…to watch the telly!" She could hardly talk. She was really drunk and weird. She was having a bad turn.

I was in the huff. I said, "There's nothing on except Dracula, and Lynn's scared."

"Where's your-yourdad?"

"He went out," I said. "I don't know where."

"I'm watching Dracula!" Mum said, giggling.

"You're not," I said.

"Mummy. I'm scared of Dracula," said Lynn.

"Youyou you're scared of Sammy! Sammy Souplefoot!"

"Shut up!" I said.

Mum got up and started walking about the room. She kept staggering. I hoped she'd fall and smash her head. She found a pair of scissors on the floor next to the mattress she and Dad slept on. She picked them up and came and sat on our bed again. She sat looking at us.

"Mummy," said Lynn.

Mum stuck out her tongue, then started singing. *"Mary needs a haircut, a haircut, a haircut…"*

She started to cut off her own hair with the scissors.

Lynn said, "Mummy."

I said, "Leave her, she's nuts."

Mum cut off more of her hair. Then she started singing, *"Now Lynn needs a haircut, a haircut, a haircut…"*

I got scared. "Shut up, you cow!"

"Please, mummy!" Lynn started to cry.

"…a haircut, a haircut, Lynn needs a haircut…" She went closer to Lynn. Lynn started screaming and hid behind her teddy.

"Fucking leave her, you cow!" I shouted so loud my throat hurt.

Mum grabbed the teddy off Lynn and started singing, *"Sammy's killing Albert, Sammy's killing Albert, Sammy's killing…"* She started ripping the teddy to bits with the scissors.

"Albert!" Lynn screamed, and dived at Mum to try to grab him back. Mum punched her in the face hard, and she fell on to her back on the bed.

I felt like I wanted to claw my arm again, but I didn't. Lynn lay there making funny noises. I stood and looked at Mum. I didn't feel mad, I was calm. I got a big mouthful of spit and I spat it right into Mum's face.

Then I went mad. I ran out into the hall screaming for Grandad, but he was already coming. He shoved me out of the way and went into the living room and I went in after him.

Mum was sitting there on the bed, singing a Barry Manilow song, "Mandy." While she was singing it, she was stabbing herself in the wrist with the scissors. It was bleeding a lot.

Grandad was scared. "Mary! Christ, Mary!" He ran over and grabbed a bit of the blanket and pressed it against Mum's wrist. "Oh, God, Mary." He looked at me. "Get dressed and get your Auntie Mae!"

Mum sang, *"Mandy, you came and you gave without taking..."*

I woke up the next morning. The grey light was coming in the windows and the bed was stained with Mum's blood and the rubbish that got thrown over Lynn. We were up nearly all night, but Lynn was awake already. She was sitting up in bed next to me, drawing in a jotter. She didn't notice I was wakened, and I lay on my side and watched her for ages. The side of her face was swollen up and her lips were twisted.

I sat up in bed. She looked at me and smiled with her twisted lips but she didn't say anything. She just kept drawing. I couldn't see what she was drawing.

I didn't say anything either. Then Grandad came in. He was wearing a dirty old suit, his best one. "Both of you awake?" he said. He had a bit of his posh voice back, but not all of it.

"Yes," said Lynn. "Did they let you see Mummy?"

"Of course they did. Your Dad's with her now."

"Is she all right?" said Lynn.

"Seems like it. They're keeping her in hospital for a week. Then she might be out."

I said, "What d'you mean, might?"

"She's acting funny. The doctor's going to have a look at her." He said to Lynn, "But she said to tell you happy birthday."

"When can I go and see her?" said Lynn.

"Tomorrow should be all right," said Grandad. "But you should try and go to sleep now. You've hardly had a wink."

"I'm not really tired."

"Well, I am. When I was your age I needed my sleep. And I still do. I'm going for a lie-down." He looked at me and Lynn as if he wanted us to say something, but we didn't. "Your Dad'll be back soon," he said. Then he went out.

"What're you drawing?" I said to Lynn.

"A picture of Mummy. It's finished now."

"Can I see it?"

She showed it to me. I didn't like it. "It's nice."

"I'm going to give it to her when I go to the hospital."

"It's nice." We didn't say anything. Then I said, "Is your face sore?"

"No. It's not sore. But I'm tired now."

"Go to sleep, then." She didn't answer me. She was nearly asleep already.

I just lay there for ages. Then I said, "D'you still wish we could live somewhere else?"

She didn't answer me. She was asleep.

"I do."

Later on, I clawed my arm a bit. But I didn't feel better. I said, "D'you want a new teddy for your birthday? I'll try and get you one. You loved Albert."

She didn't answer me. She was asleep.

"I love you."

I lay there for ages, wanting to claw my arm till I felt better, but I knew I wouldn't feel better. Then I got out of the bed. Lynn still didn't wake up.

The scissors that Mum used were lying on the floor. I got them and went back to bed.

Just before I did it, I hoped Lynn would wake up but she didn't. Then she woke up while I was doing it and she started screaming and then she stopped screaming and her blood was everywhere and I let go the scissors in her neck.

When she was dead, her blood was all over her and me and the bed, and I sat there cuddling her and saying her name and stroking her hair.

December, 1989

WHAT GOES ON

for Jim Murray

Nothing is ending, and certainly not this.
– Alexander Trocchi

ONE

Tam'd said nobody'd bother, but of course they did. Wouldn't you if you saw a ghost? They couldn't believe what they were seeing when I came into the gym. When they last saw me, I was twenty-one and looked about fifteen. Now I was twenty-four and looked forty.

"All right, Sherbo?"

"Sherbo, my man. How's it goin'?" A few said things like that to me, but the others kept on punching the bag or skipping and acted as if they hadn't seen me. Thank fuck. I went through to the changing room.

I was lacing up my training shoes when Tam came in. "All right, son? Anybody say anything?"

I shook my head.

"Good." He was a chubby man of about fifty. His speech was slurry. He used to be Scottish featherweight champion. "Just go and do what you can. Don't do too much on your first night."

"S'okay." I followed him out of the changing room into the gym. Everybody tried not to stare at me. I went over to where the big mirror was on the wall. I started to shadowbox, but I didn't like looking at myself. I looked like fucking Rumpelstiltskin. There was nobody in the ring, so I got in there and started to move around.

I could feel people looking at me, feeling sorry for me. I

threw a few punches at the air. It was easier than I'd thought it'd be. I tried to move forward fast, but the left leg wasn't much use. There wasn't much feeling in the left arm either, but I could use it all right. I shadowboxed for two rounds. It wasn't too bad, except I tripped and nearly fell twice. I wasn't going to try any skipping for a while.

I got out of the ring, put on a pair of bag mitts and knocked fuck out of the heavy bag for a round. I'd slam it with a left hook and it'd swing away, then come back at me. When it did, I'd belt it with another, then cross the right, then give it a left-right-left-right-left. By the end of the round I was fucking knackered.

Tam came over. "Call it a night, son. That'll do to break you in. Go and have a shower. You okay?"

I nodded. My voice sounded funny because of all the missing teeth, so I didn't want to talk in front of everybody. My eyes were stinging with sweat.

I had a shower and got dressed. Tam wanted to weigh me, but I wouldn't let him. I knew I was nearly nine stone, but I didn't want those cunts in the gym to know that. I was planning to fight at flyweight, the weight I'd been champion at before, which is eight stone. Next one up's bantam, which is eight and a half stone, but I didn't have the height for that. I was only five feet.

The gym was in the East End, not far from the Glasgow Meat Market. I lived in Possil, so I'd to take two buses, then walk a bit.

I'd a flat in Killearn Street, one of the worst streets up there. Nobody'd ever break into my place, though. They all knew what they'd get if I found out who it was. And I would have.

It was a smelly two-bedroom flat. I used to live in it with my girlfriend and daughter, but they'd fucked off long ago. The council just let me keep the place. I only used the one room, the smallest bedroom. It was easiest to heat. I had the telly in there, and slept on the fold-down couch. There was a bed, but the couch didn't sag so much. There was a picture on the wall, me and Margaret and Alison sitting on the grass in Kelvingrove Park.

I had two bacon rolls and a cup of tea and went to bed. I didn't mind Margaret and Alison being gone. I never liked her, she was just a shag. And the kid never seemed to have anything to do with me. Nothing really did, even before I was on smack. The only time I cared about anything was just before a fight, when I was scared I'd die. But, after it, when I knew I was all right, I never felt like it had anything to do with me.

I got up at ten in the morning and had a cup of tea and a slice of toast. Then I put on a tracksuit and jumper and training shoes and went up to the canal bank. The only running I'd done in the past three years was running away from the filth, and they'd usually caught me.

The left leg made me like fucking Hopalong Cassidy, but I ran out to Temple. It was a grey morning and it kept starting to rain and then stopping before it'd really started. So I made it out to Temple, tripping over the left leg, sweat pissing off me. I never saw anybody, thank fuck. If anybody'd laughed at the dwarf with the weird leg, I'd have drowned them in the canal after I'd booted fuck out of them.

I tried to run back from Temple, but I couldn't. So I walked. I'd have looked a right cunt taking the bus. I kept sweating all the way back to Possil.

I had a bath and something to eat, I forget what. Then I sat and read a book. My right leg felt stiff and sore, but I couldn't feel much in the left. As long as I could stand on it, I wasn't bothered.

At about five, I went down to the shop to get something else to eat. The guy in the shop, Asif, told me there'd been some bother the night before. This smackhead found out he had the AIDS virus, so he filled two syringes with his own blood and went around Possil injecting people with it. He got two or three before the filth came and got him. Asif said it was Mark Beattie. I used to know him.

TWO

It was hospital that started me off as a smackhead, and in hospital I came off it. Not that I'm blaming the hospital. I'd be better blaming Nicol Ballentine. But the only one that's to blame is me.

Nicol helped, though. A few years ago I was Western Districts Flyweight Champion, and every cunt was going on about how fucking brilliant I was. But I was into all the shit that was going up in Possil. I was fucking mental. I got into an argument with Nicol one night. He said Margaret was a cow, and I said his mother's cunt was a bit like the People's Palace—everybody in Glasgow's been there sometime. He tried to pull a blade, but I got a glass into his face first.

He lost an eye. He'd plenty of brothers, and his brothers had plenty of mates. One night they waited for me in my close. Must've been ten of them. I had a chib in my pocket, but some of them had pickaxe handles. I managed to get past them and into the back court and tried to climb over the wall, but one of them hit me with an axe handle and broke my leg. I fell off the wall, and he hit me again and broke my other leg. I got the chib —it was a flick-knife somebody'd brought me back from Italy— out of my pocket, but they were all on me and there was nothing I could do.

None of them said anything. They just got on with it. I curled into a ball as boots and axe handles got to work. Some of my teeth were stuck in my throat, choking me. Then my head seemed to splinter and I seemed to just float away.

They must have thought I was dead, and they weren't all that far wrong. I was in a coma for two months, and they thought about turning off the machine once or twice. They probably would have if it hadn't been for Margaret. She came to the hospital every day. She was pregnant with Alison, and maybe the doctors didn't want to upset her any worse by switching me off. But they told her I was a lost cause.

Maybe I was, but I wasn't a dead cause. I came out of the coma. My body was wasted from lying there for two months, and I had to learn to use my limbs all over again. They had to give me speech therapy as well, but I never managed to speak properly again. The fact that most of my front teeth were gone didn't help.

Margaret told me the filth'd got most of the cunts that did it. Thinking I was dead, they'd thrown me into the midden. That was fucking cheeky. I was found by a woman who was taking her garbage out.

I was in hospital nearly a year. My skull had been fractured, my legs had been broken, and just about everything in between had suffered some damage. You wouldn't believe the pain. I used to think I was a hard cunt, but you wouldn't believe that pain. They'd to give me morphine and stuff like that. They say morphine kills pain, but it doesn't. The pain's still there, but you don't mind it.

In the past, I'd smoked heroin, chasing the dragon, sometimes. But I'd never injected it. But in hospital I got used to being injected in the vein. And, after I got out, I'd sometimes mainline with Mark Beattie and some other smackheads I knew.

It can take you years to become an alcoholic, but becoming a smackhead's easier. Later on, in the library once, I read this book by a guy who'd been on smack. He said you'd have to shoot up twice a day for a year to get a habit. Fucking garbage. If you shot smack twice a day, you'd be addicted in a couple of weeks.

But you don't shoot up every day at first. You take a shot, then you don't for a while, then another day you shoot up again. But anybody who shoots up's well on the way to being a junkie, or he wouldn't be shooting up. At first I'd shoot up about once a week. Three months later I was a junkie, shooting smack every day.

Margaret smoked it once or twice, but she never mainlined, and she hated me for doing it. At first she tried to get me to stop it, but then she gave up and fucking ignored me. Well, she wasn't the first.

They say that if you're hooked you'll do anything to get smack, and you will. It just becomes your life. If I couldn't pay for it, I'd go and get money some way. If that meant knocking fuck out of some poor cunt, that's what it meant. But then I took some smack that the dealer'd mixed with something else—fuck knows what—and it nearly fucking killed me. For ages after that my body was totally fucked from being ill, then I realized I was permanently ill. The smack was keeping me that way, and my body couldn't fight back. I couldn't attack people anymore, so I just became a thief, and a beggar when that didn't work.

Every smackhead's a liar. You'll say anything to get it. People'd bung me money at first because they were scared of me, then later because they felt sorry for me. I think a lot of the cunts I tried to con knew they were being lied to, but still gave me money out of pity.

People have got the wrong idea about what smack does to you. Like in that film about Billie Holliday, you see them all out of their heads and happy on smack. But it's not like that. People talk about being "high" on heroin, but it's not a high, it's a stone. A smackhead who's just shot up looks a bit like he's been smoking dope, but it's not the same inside. Dope makes you think. I read books or papers when I'd been smoking dope, but smack's numbing. You just sit there, and it's everything. When you're sick for it and you put it into a vein, it hits you like an orgasm. You fucking wrench. And it takes away any interest in sex.

When I didn't have to go out looking for money, I'd just lie on the couch all day. Margaret just ignored me most of the time. She'd watch the telly or something while I lay on the couch and stuck needles in myself. She never bothered with me, or with the kid.

The fucking worst was when the Royal Wedding was on the telly, and that cunt sat watching it. The fucking room was filthy and stinking of the kid's piss and the kid was crawling about naked on the floor like a big white maggot, and she sat watching the fucking Royal Wedding. I was lying on the couch getting sick for a fix and I said something and the stupid cunt said the Royal Family all work hard and I said I know, I wonder how they manage from one fucking dinner to the next.

I knew I'd have to come off it. I'd run out of veins in my arms and was shooting it into my legs. You hear about people getting so bad they shoot it into their prick, but I've never known anybody to do that, and it wouldn't be much worse than having to do it in your legs. That's so fucking horrible. I was getting so I was running out of veins in my legs as well. I'd have to stick the needle in again and again, trying to find a vein. I knew I'd have to come off it.

I went and became a registered addict. There was this center at St George's Cross in Maryhill, and I had to go and see somebody there every morning. A lot of the time I'd get there early and they couldn't see me yet and I'd go round the corner to the Woodside library and sit in there with the old men. I'd sit there feeling terrible and trying to read a book. I must've been the most well-read cunt in Possil.

That never worked, and I started shooting up again. Margaret and I had a big fight one time when I needed smack and had no money. She'd hardly any money herself, and the giro wasn't due for days yet. I told her I wanted the money and she said she couldn't give me it, the kid had to be fed and I punched her in the face and I'd never do that and she cried and ran out the door. And then I slapped the kid because the money was getting spent on her. And she wasn't even two years old yet.

Margaret came back with two of her brothers. I think they were going to give me a doing, till they saw the state of me. One of them, Colin, just spat on my leg and said, "You're a pathetic wee cunt." Then they took the kid and left.

THREE

I went into Ruchill Hospital and came off the smack. There was no trying to come off it slowly this time. I wasn't wasting my time with that. I did withdrawal. Now I'm scared of nothing except dying and withdrawal. And I'm not sure which I'd pick.

It took me three days. I've heard about unconscious withdrawal, where they knock you out while your body comes off, but that's fucking useless. If your body came off it while you were unconscious, you'd still need it. In the three days your body's fucking puking and itching and fucking everything, but your mind's screaming for it as well. You have to decide in your mind not to take the stuff, even though you would if you could get at it.

Three days, then I could stop screaming. I felt like I used to feel, like looking through the wrong end of a telescope. I didn't know what the fuck I had to do with anything.

They discharged me from hospital. The first thing I did when I got home was dig out some pills they gave me when I was eighteen and they were treating me for not eating and not talking to anybody. The pills work, but only as a dope. They don't make you feel any better, they just turn you into a zombie for a couple of hours. You just sit around and feel nothing. I'd forgotten just how bad they were, but I took one and soon remembered. I just lay on the couch and looked at the wood-chips on the ceiling.

When that wore off, I put the pills away and didn't take them again. Margaret and Alison were gone. It didn't make any difference. When she lived with me, I still never felt like I had somebody, and I don't think she did either. Some people are born lonely.

She'd left some of the furniture, but a lot of it was gone. It was hers to take. I moved the stuff I needed into the bedroom and just stayed in there.

That was in July. It was hot and I fucking hate the heat. I didn't want to do anything. I hadn't worked since I'd left school at sixteen. There was a YTS in the park, but I chucked it after a week. Training, meant to be. Fucking laboring, only you hardly got paid for it. Fucking Government. The only ones who ever went to a Tory conference with good intentions were the IRA.

At night I just read papers or watched TV. During the day I'd just float about. There were people I'd go and see sometimes, but not many, and I didn't want to see them that often. A lot of the time I sat in the Woodside library down at St George's Cross. Now and again I'd talk to the old men who sit in there, but mostly I just read books.

A day or two before Christmas, I was in the East End, in the Barrows. It was one of those black days, pitch dark at four in the afternoon and fucking freezing. But the place was thick with people out shopping for Christmas. I wasn't interested in that, but I liked walking about down there, there being so many people and none of them knowing me. You could just float about and not be bothered.

It got so cold, I thought about getting the bus back up to Possil instead of walking. I was standing at the bus-stop at Bridgeton Cross, trying to make up my mind, when I realized Tam McGillivray was standing next to me.

He was an evil cunt. He was trainer at the Manly Art Amateur Boxing Club in the East End when he wasn't inside for assault and pushing smack. He once shoved a broken bottle up his wife's arse. Some people said he was a few coupons short of a toaster. I thought he was just an evil cunt.

I recognized him right away, but I could see he wasn't sure about me. I got pissed off just being stared at, so I said, "Hello, Tam."

"Sherbo. Thought it was you. How you doing?"

"All right. Yourself?"

"Fine. You know. Just been getting some stuff for Christmas." He had two bags. "Have you?"

"Nah." I didn't have any bags. "Just out for a walk."

"Still living up in Possil?"

I nodded.

"You've not been seen much, round and about."

"I was on smack. I'm off it now."

"I heard you were on it. How long've you been off?"

"About five months."

"You keeping all right, then?"

"Okay," I said.

"What you doing with yourself?"

"Fuck all. You know."

"You bothering with boxing at all?"

"Fuck. I'm daft enough without boxing."

"When'd you last fight?"

"About three years ago. Gordon Bonner beat me on points."

"Bonner's a good boy. He won the Western Districts this year."

"S'he still flyweight?" I asked.

"Aye. He'll win the Scottish as well. On a walkover. There'll be nobody to fight him," said Tam. There are hardly any flyweights in boxing. You don't get that many young guys small enough to weigh eight stone, and not many of them are boxers.

"Was it a walkover in the Western Districts?" I asked. A walkover's when you win the title because you're the only one who's entered at the weight.

"No. He stopped Malky Blanchard. But Malky's moved up to bantam. There'll be no flyweights in the Scottish except Bonner, unless it's some novice nobody knows about."

"Bonner'd win in that case," I said. "He's been at it too long."

Tam's bus came, but he didn't get on it. "D'you miss the game?" I knew he was going to ask me that.

"Hardly ever. Sometimes."

"Why don't you get back into it, then? You're still young."

"I'm not right since the coma." *And I want nothing to do*

with you, you cunt. "I can hardly use the left arm and leg. The smack didn't help."

"You look all right to me."

"I'm all right for pissing about. Not for fighting."

"Well, you're welcome at the club anytime. Just come down and do some training. Get yourself fit. You don't have to fight."

"Nah. If I trained, I'd want to fight."

"Come and try, then. I'm a better trainer than that cunt Creadie you were with."

"Fucking look at me, Tam."

"You look all right. You were always an ugly cunt, anyway. I'm not hassling you, son. I'm only saying if you want to come and train, you're welcome. Nobody'll bother."

"I'll see," I said.

I didn't see anybody during Christmas. I didn't put my nose over the doorstep. I wouldn't have minded seeing somebody, but I couldn't think of anybody I wanted to see, and there was nobody I knew of who'd have wanted to see me. On Christmas Day I thought of going to see this guy I'd met in hospital. We'd swapped addresses and said we'd keep in touch, but of course we didn't. You never keep in touch with somebody you met that way. And I didn't go and see him at Christmas.

New Year was about the same, but I did have one or two people come and see me. When the Manly Art Boxing Club got going again early in January, I went down and started training.

FOUR

It was as embarrassing as fuck for the first couple of weeks, going to the gym and fucking falling all over the place, and every cunt watching me. I didn't know what I was doing it for.

But it got better like Tam said it would. I never got much feeling into the left arm and leg, but I could use them. The left hand would've been crap for playing piano, but it was fucking dandy for battering people.

After a few weeks just getting fit, I started sparring. That was easier than it should've been. I was near enough fucking helpless, but the cunts I sparred with were nervous. They gave me far too much respect. They all knew it was still Sherbo they were in with, and they took it easy and tried not to hit me with anything that might annoy me.

Then it came back, and cunts started finding excuses not to spar with me. I was even easier to hit than I used to be, but I didn't give two fucks. No cunt could hurt me then and no cunt could hurt me now. I was a bit slow and clumsy because of the bad leg, but a bit of ringcraft soon took care of that. Instead of running after cunts like I used to, I started just cutting off the ring till they'd nowhere to go. Then I'd knock fucking holes in them.

Everybody in the club was taller than me—every cunt's taller than me—but that suited me. I'd crowd inside and batter fuck out of their bodies, and there was nothing they could do. No cunt anywhere ever fought better close in than I did.

Of course, I'd missed the Scottish Championships, which were held at the end of January. Bonner'd won by a walkover. I wished I'd been able to fight him, even though he'd have beaten me. I'd fought him five times. I'd stopped him twice and he'd outpointed me three times. One of my two wins was a bit dodgy, though. He was well ahead on points when we had a clinch and wrestled a bit He dislocated his shoulder—or rather I dislocated it for him—and the ref had to stop the fight.

But there was nothing dodgy about the other one. He was going well in the second round, hitting me twice every once. Then I got him with the left hook, and that was that.

But he'd spent three years becoming a better fighter and I'd spent three years being a cunt.

I finally fought in March. Tam couldn't find a flyweight, but he dug up an inexperienced bantamweight. I applied for a boxer's medical card, which you need to have or you're not allowed to box. I wasn't sure I'd get one. Until not so long ago a cripple could've got past the doctor, and quite a few did. But they've had to tighten things up because some cunts got killed. I thought having been in a coma and been on smack might've fucked things up, but I passed the medical and got the card.

The fight was on a show in the Woodside Halls in Maryhill. That was handy; a girl I'd started seeing lived just round the corner from it. She wasn't really my girlfriend, just a regular shag. She was the same age as me and had a kid. At her best she looked plain, at her worst fucking rancid. But I wasn't fucking Adonis myself.

I had dinner at her flat in the afternoon. Then she tried to give me a blow-job, but I wouldn't let her. You shouldn't when you've got a fight.

We went round to the hall at eight. As we left her flat she looked at me and said, "Young man, I think you're scared."

I wanted to scream, and for just a second I thought I was going to. Then Tam put the gumshield in my mouth and I bit down on it. I was shaking. Fighters get carried out of the ring sometimes; Tam'd nearly had to carry me in.

He was saying something but I didn't know what. My legs felt weak. The green shirt he wore seemed brighter than it was. It was like being on acid. The bell rang for the first round.

I went straight for my opponent, whose name I didn't know, winging punches like a mad bastard, trying to catch him cold. He wasn't having it. He was tall and lanky and he moved out of distance easily, snapping out a couple of jabs. I took them and kept after him. He knew his way around a ring. I kept missing with my hooks, and his left hand was scoring. It was his round.

"All right?" Tam asked me in the corner.

I sat on the stool. "Aye."

He took out my gumshield. "He caught you some sore ones."

"I'm all right."

He gave me a mouthful of water. "Your rust's showing. Your timing's off. He's outboxing you."

I knew.

"For fuck's sake crowd him. Get inside. He'll pick you off if you give him room. Chase him." He put in my gumshield.

I ran into a right to the chin at the start of the second round. It didn't hurt me, but it made him braver. He tried to stand and trade with me, letting go some good rights and lefts to my head. I rolled under them and moved in close. My left hook to the liver nearly cut him in two.

I waited in the neutral corner as the ref counted over him. I looked around me. All the colors seemed brighter. He got up at eight. The ref took a look at him, then told us to carry on.

I was in close before he knew it, hooking at his body. He grabbed and tried to hold on, but I twisted his arm and pushed him off, then battered him with four to the head. The ref dragged me away and put his arms round the guy to keep him from falling down. My right hand ached. Except for that I felt nothing.

We went round to her flat after the fight and I got the blow-job I'd missed earlier. She wanted me to stay the night, but I didn't.

On my way up to Possil, I passed by the Woodside Halls. There were still some guys sitting on the steps, drinking cans of lager. They shouted to me and I stopped for a minute and took a slug out of one of their cans.

"That was some fight, Sherbo. Fucking slaughter." It took me a while before I realized it was my fight they were talking about.

FIVE

I didn't train for a couple of weeks after that. Tam was having a bit of bother, and he couldn't be arsed with it. It was his own fault. He was a mental cunt. He worked in this garage in the East End, and him and two of his mates caught one of the other mechanics stealing. They locked the doors and told him he could have his pick: either they got the filth in and charged him or they gave him a doing. It was up to him.

The stupid cunt took the doing. Tam and his mates nearly killed him. They bashed in one side of his face and put him in a wheelchair for life. The hospital and the guy's wife got the filth in. He wouldn't press any charges or even say who'd done it, but the filth aren't always as stupid as they act. They were down at the garage talking to people and round at Tam's house trying to get him to admit to something for about a fortnight.

I kept out of it. I phoned Tam and told him I'd ring him in a week or two. I knew the mad cunt'd be all right. The filth'd never prove anything.

Somebody told me there was a bit about my fight in the *Glasgow Clarion*. I was too late to buy a copy, but I found somebody who had one. It was a report by Billy Piers, the *Clarion*'s boxing man. I used to know him; he came from Possil and was a brilliant pro lightweight not so long ago. I was surprised I hadn't noticed him at the Woodside Halls.

He gave me a good write-up, but he went on a bit about me being a smackhead. He said that after dropping off the scene completely for three years, I was back and in good form. He said the fight was "...a chilling spectacle. The dour little fighter from Possil has lost none of his almost inhuman ability to absorb punishment. He took lefts and rights flush without wobbling, and when his first left hook landed the fight was as good as over." There was a photo of me, the way I used to look.

For the fortnight I didn't see Tam, I ran every day and got

in two twenty-mile walks every week. I filled the rest of the time sitting in the library. Then I phoned Tam and he said he was feeling less hassled and we started training again.

I told him I wanted to fight Gordon Bonner. He said he didn't fancy it. "Well, who else can I fight?" I said. "There's no other flyweights about."

"There's Malky Blanchard. He's moved up to bantam, but he's really just a blown-up flyweight." I said all right, but when Tam phoned Blanchard's trainer he said he wouldn't let him fight me. Three years, for fuck's sake. I reckoned I could die and cunts'd still be scared to fight me.

Bonner it was. Tam didn't think I could beat him, but I think he was worried I'd stop coming to the gym if he didn't get me fights. He was right.

The girl I'd been seeing finished with me. She didn't say why. I wasn't bothered. The night before I fought Bonner, I didn't sleep a minute. I was scared to put the light off. I just lay on the fold-down couch and listened to the radio.

Young man, I think you're scared.

Bonner seemed bigger than I remembered, but he couldn't have been because he was still a flyweight. I didn't look at his face as I touched gloves with him. There was acne on his shoulder. It looked much redder than it should have. My balls shrank as I walked to my corner.

Tam put my gumshield in. It was wet and cold. "Work hard," he said. "Be first. Don't let him beat you to the jab. If he hurts you, get in and smother." He said something else, but the crowd drowned it out.

I looked across at Bonner. I knew what was going to happen. Bonner looked at me, and he didn't like what he saw. He'd nothing to worry about. He thought something'd changed, but I knew nothing had.

The bell rang.

November, 1989

AND I THINK TO MYSELF,
WHAT A WONDERFUL WORLD

for Bill Allsopp

The smell of shit hit him first. That was something that hadn't changed. He knew it must mean the cow could smell the death, even before anything happened. He wondered if people were the same.

Their legs shook as watery shit splashed on the ground underneath them. They were making some sort of noise, but he couldn't really hear it. He was standing with his friends some distance from where the cows were.

He'd never been inside an abattoir before, but he'd been on his way to one for a long time. He watched the men kicking and swearing at the cows and remembered the sheep.

That was when he was living in Glasgow. He'd been at a friend's flat in the East End. They'd sat up talking all night, and he'd left to go home just after dawn.

The sheep was crazy with fear, running along Duke Street in zig-zags and circles in the icy grey sunlight. Two men in white overalls came out of Melbourne Street, where the Glasgow Meat Market was. One of them shouted, "C'mere, ya cunt," and they ran after the sheep.

He watched and wondered if it had run off as they were unloading it from a lorry, or if it had somehow escaped from the Meat Market as they were about to kill it.

They chased it from one side of Duke Street to the other. It didn't make any noise, and he remembered that in dreams of the same kind he was always too scared to scream. He'd just run with his legs seeming to vibrate, like the sheep was doing.

And it was the stuff of his nightmares—alone and on the run in a city where nobody's on your side and everybody wants to see you captured and killed. He thought of science fiction films he'd seen.

He didn't see them catch the sheep. Its panic-run took it back down Melbourne Street, towards the Meat Market, and they ran after it. He knew that was the end of it, but it would have been anyway.

He walked over to the corner of Melbourne Street. His feet were numb with cold and he walked stiffly. The sheep and the men had disappeared round the corner. There was some sheep-shit on the ground. He found some more in Duke Street. He couldn't imagine how it could shit and run at the same time. Then he remembered his dreams again.

Glasgow was four years ago. He could smell the shit of the cows. Then a man in bloody white overalls came over and said, "D'you want to see me drop one?"

None of his friends said anything. He'd had to talk the three of them into coming along with him.

"You're going to do it anyway," he said to the man. The man didn't answer. "All right. Let's have a look," he said. He followed the man over to where the smell of quivering cow-shit was stronger. His friends followed him.

They watched a cow be humanely slaughtered. One of the men put electrodes to its head. It gave a screaming snort and staggered, but didn't fall. It was still standing when the knife opened its throat. It fell to the concrete floor, kicking and spraying piss and shit and blood. They opened its belly with an axe, then scraped out its insides. By then it had stopped kicking and the blood was splashing rather than spraying. The body was covered with shit.

Two of his friends went outside to vomit. His other friend went with them. He stayed where he was. He felt sick, but his stomach felt fine.

The smell of shit was much stronger. He went back to where he'd been standing, at the far end of the abattoir. He waited for his friends to finish being sick and come back in.

More cows died the same way. He watched and thought of the holocaust.

One of the men in stinking overalls came over to talk. "Nothing gets wasted," he said. "Nothing at all. We even use the lips and the eyelids. They go in the sausages."

He nodded and didn't answer. The man went on, "You should see what we do to a sheep sometimes. We all put a pound into a kitty. Then we let the sheep run about the place, and we chase it with knives. First one to cut its dick off gets the money."

He left with his friends. One of them said that people who ate meat were cruel and stupid. He agreed.

He knew it'd be a few weeks before his friends' stomachs would let them eat meat again. There was bacon in his fridge and he was going to have it for dinner that night. And then no more.

October, 1989

BODILY FUNCTIONS

He saw her twenty years later, when he went back to Glasgow for a holiday. It was in a pub in Maryhill. He was standing at the bar, and she was coming out of the toilet. He wondered if she'd wiped her arse.

That wasn't his only thought, of course. There was surprise and the familiar regret, and a bit of hurt when she didn't seem to recognize him. He hoped fifteen years in the Australian sun hadn't weathered him that badly.

He watched as she sat town with a man, probably her husband.

"What's up?" his nephew said to him. It was his nephew who'd brought him to this pub. It was the first time they'd seen each other since he'd emigrated.

"That's an old girlfriend of mine sitting over there," he said. He took a mouthful of Grouse and water. "Twenty years since I last saw her."

His nephew looked interested. "You sure it's her?"

He nodded. "She's hardly changed. I recognized her as soon as I saw her. Doesn't seem to know me, though."

"That's a long time. Must've been pretty heavy for you to remember her."

He nodded again. "It was."

He was in his mid-twenties, working as a jobbing joiner. She lived by herself in a tenement flat in Maryhill. It was a room and kitchen with an outside toilet that she shared with five of her neighbors.

He lived with his parents nearby. He had a key to her flat, and on his way to work each morning, he'd let himself in and make breakfast for them both. There was a dairy just next to her close, and he'd stop in there for rolls, butter and milk.

It suited them both. It suited her to be wakened with breakfast, and it suited him to find her in bed. They never said it, but they both thought they were in love and would probably get married some day.

One night, Glasgow had one of the worst storms it'd known. Wind and rain got together to give the city as uncomfortable a night as it could hope not to have, and it lasted till about five in the morning. At six-fifteen, as usual, he went to the dairy for breakfast.

He let himself into her flat without waking her, and went to the kitchen. He got a knife from a drawer and buttered the rolls with it. Then he went to put the knife in the sink to be washed, and love came to an end.

Sitting majestically in the sink was the biggest crap he'd ever seen. There wasn't much of a smell from it. He stood and looked at it and imagined her squatting over the sink, giving birth to it.

Knowing that what he was doing was ludicrous, he crept out of the flat without waking her. He closed the door gently, dropped the key through the letter box and went to work.

He could only suppose that the storm had made the thought of the walk to the outside toilet too much for her. He hoped she'd planned to clean up before he arrived and had just overslept. But—he couldn't help but think it—could she have thought he wouldn't mind?

He avoided her for a fortnight, then finally wrote her a letter saying he'd met somebody else. The truth sounded too stupid, even to him.

February, 1990

HOLDING BACK THE DAWN

All I can see
is you walking away from me
and I'm too scared to say please stay, please stay –
don't go away

I'll carry a torch for you
until my fingers burn
and speak your name
but only in a whisper
because it's almost over,
almost gone
and I'm still here
—all smiles and blisters

Steve Jinksi

It started in the bathroom. Before that, Tom had been watching TV in the living room and she had been feeding the cat in the kitchen. It was just after midnight. They were the only ones in the flat.

Kate was coming out of the kitchen when Tom went into the bathroom and locked the door. She pressed her face against the frosted glass panel on the door and shouted, "Mind if I watch you?"

Tom laughed and opened the door. "Piss off." He shoved her back a bit.

"Can't I watch? There's nothing on the telly."

"Piss off." He went back into the bathroom and she went to the living room.

"My turn," she said, heading for the bathroom as he came out of it. She went in and closed the door.

"My turn too," he said, pressing his face against the glass.

She laughed. "Pervert! Piss off."

He laughed and stayed where he was.

"Come on," she said. He didn't move. "Tom!"

"Hurry up. Get on with it."

"Come on, piss off. I'm going to burst."

She opened the door and pushed him away. He pressed his face to the glass as soon as she'd gone back in.

"Tom! Don't. I really need a piss."

"Go on, then," he said.

"Piss off! You can't see anything through that glass anyway."

"You can. You've got to find a little bit and look through. I can see you. I should see more in a minute."

She believed him. His face was so close to the glass that his nose was flat and white. "This isn't funny," she said.

He laughed.

"I'm going to do it anyway," she said.

"Goody."

She couldn't do it. She opened the door and he backed away, grinning. "Come on, fuck off," she said. "This is getting out of hand."

"You started it."

"I was just having a laugh! I let you go."

He didn't say anything.

"Are you going to let me go?" she said.

He grinned at her.

"Bastard."

She went back into the bathroom and it happened again. She opened the door and he backed off. She was furious.

"Tom, I'm going to wet myself."

He smiled.

"I am!"

"Go and use the bog, then."

She went inside and he stuck his face to the glass again.

"Tom!" She was nearly in tears as she opened the door.

"What the *fuck* are you doing?"

He looked surprised. "Sorry, I thought you knew. I'm looking at you through the glass every time you try to have a piss."

"God." Her bladder felt ready to give in. She slid down the wall and sat there on the floor in a fetal position.

"Want a cushion?" said Tom. She didn't answer. He sat down facing her on the floor, crossing his legs.

Kate started to cry. She closed her eyes to hide it, but the tears squeezed out. "This is hell," she murmured.

"Hell? Nah. It's just life. Life's like that. Frustrating. Like why I'm always late for work. I wake up in plenty of time. But of course, not unlike yourself right now, I need to go to the toilet. But, as you know, I like a cup of tea first thing in the morning, and I can never make up my mind whether to go to the kitchen and put the kettle on and then go to the toilet, or go to the toilet first. I lie there and think about it for so long, I'm never out of bed in time for work."

Kate had stopped crying. "Stop it. Please. It's just stupid."

He farted loudly. "Pardon me. Don't worry, my arse is ozone-friendly."

She dosed her eyes again, but not to cry. "Grow up."

"Did you see the *Sunday Sport* last week?" he said. She didn't answer. He didn't expect her to. "Naturally, I didn't buy it. Have you noticed nobody ever seems to buy it? They all just happen to have read a friend's copy. Anyway, I actually didn't buy it. Somebody at the home had a copy."

Kate had started to cry again.

"They're into biology, these days. This doctor's discovered that the texture of raw liver's the same as the human vagina. Seems his butcher does a roaring trade. There was a really informative article—'101 Things To Do With Liver Before You Eat It.'" He waited. Kate went on crying. "Aren't you going to ask how Sean's liver's doing?"

She sniffled. "How is Sean?"

"Dying, of course. Apparently that's what liver cancer does

to you. Lucky he's blind, or we'd have to tell him not to start reading any long novels."

She cried harder.

"Why don't you come back and see him?" said Tom. "It'd mean a lot to him."

"If you don't let me go to the toilet, I'm going to phone the police."

He threw back his head and roared, slapping his thighs theatrically. "Do it! Please! I want to see their faces when they arrive and you tell them what the problem is."

"You really are a bastard." Her voice was raspy from crying. "I'm going to *wet* myself. If you had the slightest bit of *kindness*—"

"You wouldn't know kindness if you found it floating in your discharge," he told her.

"The Patron Saint of Self-Righteous Wankers hath spoken," she said through her teeth. "Working in a children's home makes you St Francis of fucking Assisi and everybody else is just evil —"

"No. Just you," he said. She didn't answer. "Actually, Sean'd probably sympathize with you right now. He knows what it's like when you have to piss in front of people. He sits in his chair and pisses himself all day."

"That's nothing to do with me."

"Oh, for fuck's sake! Whose fucking business is it, then? His parents never come near him. He's blind, he can't walk and now he's fucking dying! He's only thirteen."

"Why don't I just go and visit every kid in the home?" she sobbed. "Would that keep you happy?"

"Yeah. Why don't you? But you should at least go and see Sean. He's asked me about you."

"I don't believe you."

"He has. I swear it. He really liked you. What am I supposed to say to him? 'Well, Sean, I'm afraid the girl you were talking to won't be coming back. You see, she'd just dropped in to see me, and she only spoke to you to pass the time because I was busy. And, as a matter of fact, I won't be seeing much more of her, since she's about to head off to Germany with the DHSS's answer to Samuel Beckett.'"

Suddenly, he started to cry. "I love you, you stupid, vicious cunt."

At three in the morning, she started to wet herself and managed to stop.

"You'd be best to go to the toilet," Tom said. "Holding it in this long's bad for your bladder or something like that."

"Fuck off." Her voice was a miserable whisper.

"What time's Mike picking you up?"

"Quarter to six."

"Uh-huh. Dawn start to the journey. Very romantic. Well, you'd better go to the bog. Might put him off if you wet yourself just before he arrives."

"Will you let me go, then?"

He looked at his watch. "I'll have to, eventually," he said sadly.

March, 1990

QUARTET:

LET NOTHING YOU DISMAY

Short of being terminally ill and knowing it, there's probably no feeling worse than having no secure home. I'm not talking about being homeless, I'm talking about being threatened in the place where you live.

Bedsits are substitutes for homes, but some are better substitutes than others. The one I lived in during my first three months in Edinburgh wasn't too bad. Then the landlord sold it and I'd to move out in a hurry.

I'd a lot on my plate at the time, and couldn't fit in the hassle of looking at many other places. I didn't know anybody in Edinburgh who could help me look, so I just took the first place I found. It was a bedsit in Newington, the sort of place you wipe your feet on the way out of. The furniture was falling apart, the carpet had huge holes in it, and the window gave an enchanting view of the decayed wall across the street. Rats would have raised the tone of the place.

I moved in on a Saturday night in February. I had flu and it was freezing. The central heating was on a white meter system, meaning that it came on now and again, but the room was like a fridge the rest of the time.

I took off my shoes and got into the sagging bed fully clothed. I lay there for about two hours, trying to keep warm and read a book and not quite managing to do either. At around ten there was a knock on the door of my room.

I felt shivery and stiff as I got up and opened the door. The guy who stood there was about eighteen. He looked nervous.

"Hi," he said. "Could you do me a favor?" I just looked at him. "I've got to go out for half-an-hour. Can you listen for anybody at my door?"

"How come?" I said.

He started to whisper, looking around the hall. I stepped back and motioned to him to come into my room. He did. "It's the girl in the room next to mine—Emma, her name is. She's only sixteen. Comes from a scheme, Pilton or somewhere. She's hardly ever here, but she gives the keys to her room to these guys, little headcases from the scheme . . ."

"Been giving you hassle?" He looked the sort who got bullied at school.

"They haven't threatened me. But they keep picking the lock on my room door when I'm out and taking stuff."

"Are you sure?"

"Yeah. The lock's covered in scratches."

"Have you said anything to them?"

"No," he said. "There's too many of them." He'd have been scared shitless if there'd only been one. "Anyway, I'm moving out on Monday. If you could just listen for half-an-hour—"

"All right."

He was gone for twenty minutes and I didn't hear anyone go to his door. I sat on my bed and shivered and thought. When he came back we sat in my room and talked for ten minutes.

His name was Jeff. I asked if he'd told the dumplord about the bother he'd had. "No," he said. "I couldn't prove anything, and they'd fucking kill me for it."

"How many're in there tonight?"

"Three or four. That's the usual lot, anyway. I haven't seen them tonight. Just heard them."

I thought a little more, then told Jeff, "I'm going out for ten minutes. Keep an eye on my door."

I put on my shoes and coat and went downstairs to the payphone on the corner. There was a phone in the flat, but like phones in many Edinburgh bedsits, it only took incoming calls.

I rang a friend in Glasgow, where I'd lived until three months earlier. "Do me a favor," I told him. "Phone me at midnight, will you? Yeah. But I won't answer the phone. I'll tell you when I see you. Yeah. Thanks." I hung up and went back to my bedsit.

Jeff said nobody'd gone to my door. I said goodnight to him, went into my room and locked the door. Then I switched off the light and sat down in a chair to wait.

My friend's phone call came at midnight, just as I'd asked. I heard a room door opening, then a babble of young, drunk voices and the sound of Bros in the background. The phone was picked up, and one of them repeated my name and told my friend to wait a minute. Then there was a knock on my door.

I sat where I was, trying not to breathe too loud. There were a few harder knocks and they shouted my name. I didn't answer. I heard them tell my friend I wasn't in and hang up. Then, as I knew they would, they came back to my door.

"He must be in," one of them said. "His key's in the door." So they were looking through the keyhole.

There was a furious knocking on the door and one of them roared my name. "He must be oot," I heard another say.

That's right, you morons. I'm out. That's why the key's in the lock. I shinned down the drainpipe and went for a pint. I'm coming back the same way. You Edinburgh retards.

I listened to the scratching sound of them trying to pick my lock. I didn't think they'd be able to. Unlike the antique on Jeff's door, this wasn't a bad lock.

The scratching went on for a minute or two, and I heard one of them say "Shite!" Then my door was kicked in.

One kick did it, and it threw me. I hadn't expected it. Two of them came into the room. My eyes were well-adjusted to the dark, but they didn't see me. I was on them before they realized I was there.

One of them was reaching for the lightswitch. I hit him in the face and he fell without a sound. I grabbed the other and wrestled him against the wall. "The cunt's in here!" he shouted as we struggled. He was strong. I got my thumbs into his eyes and pressed. The scream he let out must have put a scare into the ones who were out in the hall. I heard them open the front door and slam it behind them.

I let go of the guy and he went down on his knees. His mate was getting up. I gave him a kick in the head and he went back down. I turned on the light and had a look at them. They were aged about sixteen or seventeen. The one I'd gouged was crying. The other was bleeding from his nose and scalp and looked ready to cry.

I didn't say anything. I didn't want my voice to let them know how shaken I was. I kicked them out of my way, went out and pulled the broken door shut behind me.

I got hold of myself and went and knocked on Jeff's door. "Jeff!" I called. No answer. I knocked again. No answer. "Jeff! It's me. I know you're in. Open the door or I'll fucking kick it in!"

He opened the door. He was dressed and hadn't been sleeping. He looked scared. "What's up?"

"Don't worry," I said. My voice sounded high. "D'you know the landlord's phone number?"

"Yeah."

"Get out and phone him. Tell him those cunts broke into my room. Then call the police."

He looked terrified as he went. Back in my room, I found my guests sitting on the bed. One of them had streaming red eyes.

"Do me a favor," I said harshly. "Try to get out of here. Please."

"I cannae see," Red-Eyes bleated.

"Good. I hope you're blind for life. I was trying to poke them right out."

The dumplord and the pigs arrived together. Jeff was the last to get back. He'd been so scared he'd gone for a walk.

I struck lucky—one of the pigs was that rare animal, a policeman who isn't half-witted. I didn't have to repeat myself a dozen times as I explained what'd happened.

"Jeff told me they'd been getting into his room while he was out. I've got stuff in there—papers and stuff—I can't afford to lose. If they were going to try to get into my room, I wanted to know about it. So I got a friend to phone me, but I didn't answer it so they'd think I was out..."

The dumplord, Muir, evicted the girl who had the room when she came back next day. Muir happened to be a woodwork teacher, so he was able to make a fair job of repairing my door. He did that in the afternoon. That night, very late, he was back.

"Thought I'd better let you know," he told me. "I've just had a phone call from the police. Jeff's in hospital. Intensive care. Somebody kicked the shite out of him tonight. Just down the road, outside the Odeon. Fractured his skull."

"Did the police get them?"

"No. It'll be mates of those wee wankers. Giving it to Jeff for telling you about them. You'd better watch yourself. Those wee cunts're dangerous."

He was right. There are any number of people whose business or inclination is to kill people. But they're less frightening than a dozen drunk teenagers who're liable to kill you out of sheer stupidity, when they start kicking you and forget to stop.

"You'd better watch," Muir said again. "They'll be back here for you."

November, 1989

THAT SUMMER

ONE

Jay was as ordinary as her name. I met her ar a time when people were trying to kill or maim me, and I shared a flat with her for a few months.

The place was in Stockbridge, in the New Town. I was lucky to find it. I'd had to move out of my bedsit in Newington before the local headcases gave me something elastoplast wouldn't fix. I answered an ad in the *Evening News* and went to view the room in the shared flat with the marks of my most recent scuffle still on my face.

I didn't expect to get the room. It was a big, bright room in a huge flat in the most desirable area of Edinburgh. The rent was reasonable and I knew there'd be no shortage of people wanting it.

I was shown round by Ian, Jay's boyfriend, who she shared a room with. Then I sat in the living room for a while and talked with Ian, Jay and the other two who lived in the flat, Stewart and Debbie. We got along all right, but I didn't think they were bowled over by me. Jay was lovely and dark-haired and long-limbed. She didn't say much, just sat cuddling the cat, whose name she said was Jenny.

They told me they still had people to see, but they'd phone and let me know one way or the other.

Ian rang next day to say they'd picked me. "The lease doesn't start officially till next week," he said. "But, since you're having so much bother up there, you can move in tomorrow if you like. The room's empty."

So I did. I packed my stuff and moved out of Newington without even telling the dumplord. He still had my deposit, so he wasn't losing money.

I reckon the others in the flat thought they'd made the

wrong choice after I first moved in; I hardly came out of my room for a fortnight. I had a stink of violence about me that I was afraid other people could actually smell, and knowing how stupid that was didn't change it.

After a couple of weeks I felt better. I'd just been suffering from a serious case of having lived in a dump, and it wore off. Instead of sitting in my room reading or working all the time, I'd spend the cool April afternoons walking by the Water of Leith or shopping in Stockbridge. I liked the area. It was like the West End of Glasgow, with better architecture and without the community spirit.

Most nights I'd sit in the living room and read or watch TV with the others, or, more often, with Jay, Debbie and Stewart. Ian said he hated TV for "pandering to the crassness of public taste" and spent most evenings sitting upstairs reading.

Jay was so warm. When you brushed against her she didn't draw away like most people would. She stayed where she was, accepting your accidental nearness. She had a funny little magnet inside her that could draw people like steel shavings, and she was more shy and unsure of herself than anybody I'd ever met.

I got to know her just through spending a lot of time alone with her in the living room. Stewart, who was a student, spent a lot of his evenings studying in the library. Debbie was keeping herself busy having an affair with a married man, and Ian was usually upstairs reading Nietzsche or something.

Jay was twenty-five, a year older than me. She came from some pissy little backwater outside Edinburgh, but she'd left when she was seventeen to study ceramics at Edinburgh Art College. In the three years since leaving college, she'd been painting unsuccessfully and working at various casual jobs. At present she worked part-time in a local second-hand clothes shop. She'd met Ian at college. She'd been going out with him for five years, and living with him for two.

Since Ian had left college, he'd been making sculptures that were about as successful as Jay's paintings. They lived together in a state of continual, constant poverty that I'd never known. I was often painfully short of money. But I'd go through periods of being broke and periods of more or less getting by. Ian and Jay didn't. Their lifestyle was to be constantly broke. In April the nights were still cold, but they couldn't afford to put on the central heating in their room. Jay told me they accepted that in winter they just had to freeze.

One night I went for a drink with her. We sat in the Antiquary Bar in St Stephen's Street, just round the corner from the flat. We both got drunk and Jay said to me, "I really like having you to talk to."

"Same here."

"I don't really have any other friends I can talk to," she said. "Maureen's about the closest, but even she never listens. She tells me all her problems, but she never listens to mine. When I was out with her last week, she went on about her own problems for ages. Then she said to me, 'I don't want our friendship to be a one-sided thing, with me using you as a sounding-board all the time. If you ever need to talk, you know I'll listen.' So I started to tell her some things, and she just carried on about herself." She laughed her shy, embarrassed laugh. "I'm just whingeing."

"Doesn't sound like whingeing," I said. I wasn't aware that I'd ever played therapist to her; she'd told me vaguely that she and Ian were having problems, and that she was upset by her parents' offhand attitude towards her (and she had a point there—as a kid, she'd rebelled by going to school, since her folks were happy to let her stay off when she liked), but there hadn't been much else.

"I hadn't noticed you talking about yourself that much," I said.

"More to you than to anybody else. Like I say, I appreciate having you there. You always listen."

"S'what I'm there for." I was pleased.

She smiled at me. "Funny thing is, when you came round to look at the room, I took one look at you and thought, 'No chance.'"

"How come?"

"You looked like a cross between an ex-Fettes schoolboy and a mass murderer."

"Thanks."

"But then when we were all talking to you, I changed my mind. I more or less decided, even though we'd people still to see."

"I didn't realize at the time. I didn't expect to be picked."

"I know," she said. "We could all see that."

The next day I had to go to Glasgow. There was somebody there who depended on me and was having problems. I stayed nearly a week, then got a bus back to Edinburgh.

I arrived at the flat at noon. There was nobody else in. I knew Jay was at work. I was sitting in the living room reading when Ian came in. "Hi," I said.

"Hi," he said. He was a thin, nervy little man with oily black hair and a pointed ginger beard. His clothes were nearly always brown or grey.

"Back from Glasgow?"

No, I'm still there, I thought. "Yeah. Got back about half-an-hour ago."

"What's that you're reading?" he asked.

I held up the book "*Chronicle of a Death Foretold*. It's not bad."

"I don't read much modern fiction," he said. "The only novelists I like are Dostoevsky and Thomas Mann." I wondered if that was why he looked and dressed like Raskolnikov. "All other writers are just inconsequential "

I looked to see if he was joking, and realized he wasn't. I didn't say anything, and when he went upstairs to read *Faustus* or play his double bass or jerk off or something, I went out for a walk.

I followed the Water of Leith out to Dean Village, then came back the same way. I wandered around Stockbridge for a while, then went to the shop where Jay worked. She called it Hippy Fashions because of the stuff it sold.

Either she was delighted to see me or she did a good job of faking it when I went in. "Hi! I didn't think you'd be back from Glasgow yet." She was wearing a fringed skirt and a black top. She looked beautiful.

"I just got back," I said. "I've just been talking to the Raskolnikov of Robertson Circus." I shook my head.

She smiled unhappily. "You don't like Ian, do you?"

"I don't dislike him. But he gives me a pain in the arse." I told her what he'd said that day.

She nodded. "That's Ian. He thinks everything he says should be written on a stone tablet. But he's not always like that."

"You mean he's not always a wanker?"

"He's not. You really don't know him. He is getting worse, though. He's always been arrogant, but these days he thinks all his likes and dislikes should be taken like a message from the Pope. You're scared to ask him what he takes in his coffee in case he says"—she put on a fair imitation of Ian's voice—"*I never take milk, it's bad for the intrinsic values in my sculptures!*"

"*All milk is inconsequential!*" I waved my hands like Ian did when he was holding forth.

Jay became serious. "But he is a nice guy. You should give him a chance. He likes you. D'you want some tea?"

"Yeah, please."

She went into the back shop and put the kettle on. A customer came in and began to browse. Jay came back with two mugs of tea and handed me one. We didn't speak much until the guy'd bought a shirt and a brooch and left.

"Ian's one of the reasons I'm glad you moved into the flat," Jay told me. "When you're living with him, it's easy for him to make you think he's right. He kept telling me I should read Dostoevsky and listen to Beethoven. So I did, but I couldn't get into it. But he was able to make me think there was something wrong with me, and something wrong with the books and music I liked. But eventually I thought, I shouldn't let him dictate to me. I knew that if I told him he should read Patrick Suskind or listen to Michelle Shocked, he wouldn't. So I wasn't going to be what he wanted me to be."

TWO

Ian Munning wasn't a person, he was a caricature. He was the archetypal failed artist. I could sympathize to a certain extent; I used to be a failed writer. But he felt, in his Nietzsche-reading, apolitical, arrogant way, that the world owed him success and was lucky to have him living in it. I know nothing about sculpture and couldn't judge his work, but he often told me that public taste was so poor that his greatness probably wouldn't be recognized for years to come.

He saw himself as being beyond politics, and said he didn't care what the Government or anybody else did as long as signing on the dole brought him enough to live on. He was in love with the romantic image of the impoverished artist. His parents paid the rent on his studio.

He was the consummate pseudo-intellectual. Jay described him as opinionated, but she was wrong. He had no opinions of his own, he just memorized other people's from books.

One night, Stewart and I were watching TV. Jay was staying the night with her parents in the middle of nowhere. Ian came in and asked us if we'd like to go for a drink with him. He'd just finished a sculpture he was pleased with.

Stewart made some excuse. I was about to do the same, when I thought of Jay telling me to give him a chance.

We went to the Antiquary. It was awkward at first. I didn't have much to say to him. I mentioned that I'd been helping to look for bodies after an explosion in a village on the Scottish borders six months earlier. The disaster'd been such headline news that even Ian had heard about it.

"Did you find any bodies?" he asked me.

"I found bits of bodies. The explosion from the factory'd seen to the area for about a quarter of a mile each way. There were a couple of corpses left in one piece, but I didn't find them."

"Christ. What was it like?"

"It's a funny feeling," I said. "It really brings death home to you. You find part of a torso or something, and you look at the people with you and realize that the bit of meat was the same. It walked around like that too, before it got blown up. But it doesn't really horrify you, 'cause whole, living people and a piece of a corpse don't seem to have anything to do with each other, even though you know they do."

He nodded. "Death is something we can't even begin to imagine," he said.

"I don't know," I said. I was as eloquent as I always am after four pints of Guinness and a Southern Comfort. "It depends on what you think death is. Whether you've got any religion. If you think the body's just a sort of organic machine, then death's just not existing, like it was before you were born. I'd think not existing's easy enough to imagine."

He looked uneasy. Then he said, or rather recited, "No. Death is something we can't even begin to imagine." And I realized he was just regurgitating something he'd read in one of his books on philosophy.

"You should write that on the wall of the bog," I told him. I didn't argue any more. I'd have been as well arguing with the book he was quoting from. However well you argue with a printed page, the print on it won't change. And Ian and a piece of paper had about equal ability to think for themselves. To Ian, 2+2=4 and death is something we can't even begin to imagine.

Stewart was still in the living room when I got back to the flat. Ian had gone for a walk. I made some tea and sat glowering at the TV.

"Are you all right?" Stewart finally asked me.

"Yeah. Why?"

He shook his head. "I'm not blind. I don't know why you let Ian get you so wound up. The guy's a pathetic little nonentity."

I took a slurp of tea. "There's nothing wrong with him that being garrotted wouldn't fix."

I went to bed wondering if Ian knew how angry he'd made me. If he did, he hadn't shown it.

Just before we'd left the pub, he'd started talking about Jay. "She's a lot more intelligent than you'd think just to speak to her," he said.

"I think she's as bright as anybody I've met," I said. *And a thousand times smarter than you, you elitist little lamebrain.*

He made a face. "Yeah, she's not stupid. But she's more intelligent than she seems. But she doesn't really show it. Intellectually she just drifts. I've tried telling her what she should read and listen to, but she won't persevere long enough to understand it."

I didn't hit him, but looking back now I think I should have.

THREE

A few weeks later, Jay became depressed. She wouldn't say what was wrong, and I wondered if I had anything to do with it. I certainly hadn't helped. Knowing how much she liked talking to me, I'd been spending most of my time in Glasgow.

One night she asked if I'd like to go for a walk. I said okay, and we walked by the Water of Leith. It was now early June, and the night was warm and heavy. Jay wore jeans and a T-shirt and her dark hair was tied back.

"What's up with you?" I asked.

"Just fed up."

"About what?"

"You name it," she said. "I'm not too bad now. I've made up my mind about some things. But I was really down. I could've done with you being around."

"Sorry. But I had to be in Glasgow."

"I know."

We walked a bit more. Then I said, "So what've you made up your mind about?"

"I'm giving myself another year to get somewhere as an artist. If I haven't managed it by then, I'm going to give in and do something else."

"How come?"

"I actually don't like being broke all the time. It doesn't really bother Ian—"

"He enjoys it," I said.

"Shut up. He doesn't." She looked at me and went on. "He doesn't mind it, though. But I do. I don't like freezing to death because I can't afford the heating. And not being able to paint sometimes because I haven't enough money for materials."

"Good," I said.

"Why's it good?"

"Because I don't like you freezing."

I didn't have much time of my own during the next month or so. Some work I'd done was being featured by a small theater at the Edinburgh Festival Fringe in August, and I was tied up with rehearsals most of the time. I still managed to go out for a drink with Jay a couple of times a week. And the effect that was having would have told a more sensible man to find some distance and keep it.

About a week before the show went on, I was at a rehearsal in the afternoon. Tempers were so short as to be non-existent. The actors and the director were sick of each other, and they were all sick of me. I decided to leave them to sort things out.

I didn't want to go back to the flat. I was in a foul mood, and the bustle of tourists in the town didn't soothe me. I wandered through bookshops and record shops, understanding for the first time why so many Edinburgh people flee to Glasgow during the Festival. Eventually I walked down to Stockbridge and, after a calming walk by the river, went along to Hippy Fashions.

I wasn't sure whether Jay would be working there that day, but she was. There were no customers, and I found her reading a book.

She was pleased to see me. She made some tea and asked what'd happened to the rehearsal.

"It's still going on," I said. "The actors and the director all fell out. The only thing they could agree on was that I was giving them all a pain in the arse. I thought I'd better get out of the way and let them get on with it."

She laughed. "It'll work out. You'll be surprised at how good it is on the night."

"Yeah." I perched on the edge of the counter and said, "Listen. There's something I want to talk to you about."

"Let's hear it," she said. Of course, at that point customers started arriving. "Well?" Jay said to me as she served them.

"I'll tell you later," I said.

I stayed in the shop all afternoon. It stayed busy. My mood got better. Jay kept covering her face to stifle her laughter as I tried to convince a middle-aged woman that a ridiculous Davy Crockett hat suited her. She actually believed me and bought it.

"Is that your boyfriend?" the woman asked Jay as she paid her for the hat.

"No," said Jay.

After the woman left, Jay laughed and hugged me. "You *bastard*," she said with tender fury. "I thought she'd see me laughing. You were so *sincere*."

I grinned at her. "She bought the hat, didn't she? Can I have your job?"

Later, as she was locking up the shop, she said, "I thought you had something to tell me."

"I have."

"Tell me, then."

I did. She'd guessed already.

The show wasn't great, but it was better than it could have been. It ran for a week. The reviews were shit. Jay came along on the third day, and we went for a drink afterwards.

We picked a place called the Black Bull. I'd heard it used to be a hang-out of Robert Burns, Robert Louis Stevenson and Burke and Hare. From the reviews of my stuff, I reckoned I was probably closest to the last two.

"Maureen phoned me this morning," said Jay, after I'd got the drinks. "She's convinced there's something going on between us. She said every time she phones me, I'm out with you."

"What'd you think of the show?" I said.

"Good. But you know it's good." I didn't say anything. "How're you feeling?" she asked me.

"All right. I'm not going to top myself."

"I should jolleigh well hope not, deah boy." She'd affected a horsey English accent. "There's an *awrt* to killing oneself, a positive awrt. That's what my Uncle Algernon said just before he topped himself Hawr-hawr-*hawr!*"

I forced a smile, knowing how weak it looked.

Jay stopped clowning. "I do love you," she said. "You do believe that, don't you?"

I nodded.

"Does it hurt you when I say that?"

"What d'you *think?*" I said. Suddenly, my eyes were stinging. Jay took my hand. "What're you *doing* with that clown?"

"I'm really sorry," she said. She let go of my hand.

FOUR

I kept out of her way for the next week. Then, on the last day of the Festival, Stewart decided to have a party in the flat—for occupants only—to watch the firework display at Edinburgh Castle. We'd be able to watch it from our attic window. I was too beaten to find an excuse not to be there.

Ian, Jay, Stewart, Debbie and myself all took glasses of red wine up to the attic and sat on the floor with the light off. We had a radio on, and we listened to live commentary on the firework display as we watched it from the window. In the dark, I was aware of Jay's warm presence beside and slightly behind me, lightly pressing against my left shoulder.

And I wanted to feel more, all of her, hair, skin, breasts, buttocks, cunt. I wanted to feel.

When the fireworks were over, Ian said, "Let's go downstairs." His voice scraped the darkness like a knife scraping across a plate. I didn't want to move. But I had to.

We sat at the kitchen table in candlelight and had more wine. Stewart rolled a joint. Jay was sitting opposite me. Ian was pontificating about something, but I didn't listen to whatever it was. Jay was quite drunk, and when Stewart passed her the joint, it hit her right away. Smiling, she closed her eyes and hung her head so her dark hair fell forward, shadowing her face.

I had to stop myself from shivering. *You are so lovely,* I thought. *And what am I going to do?*

The next day, I was sitting in the living room talking to Stewart. Jay was there, but she wasn't saying much. Then Ian came in.

He was just out of bed and hadn't combed his hair. He looked pale. He walked over to where I was sitting on the couch and stood in front of me. "Get up," he said quietly.

"What?" I said. Stewart had stopped talking.

Jay said, "Ian."

"Get up," said Ian.

"What for?" I said.

"I can't hit you while you're sitting there," he said.

"I don't get this," I said.

"Ian, stop it," said Jay.

"For fuck's sake," said Stewart.

"Get fucking up!" Ian said to me, a specter of vengeance in a grey dressing gown.

"I don't get this," I said again. "I'm not getting up."

"Fucking scared?"

"Yeah," I said.

He raised his fist. "Get up."

"Fuck off."

A couple of days after that, I phoned an old contact of mine who lived in Inverness. For a long time he'd been asking me to go up there and work with him on a project of his. I told him I'd be up there as soon as I could.

I made the call on a Wednesday. I moved out of the flat the following Sunday. All I took with me was a big holdall. I'd arranged for a friend to pick up the rest of my stuff and either store it for me or send it up to Inverness.

My bus was at seven in the evening. At six, I went into the living room to say goodbye to Stewart. Ian and Jay were upstairs. I didn't know where Debbie was, but I seldom did.

Stewart looked at my holdall. "You off, then?"

"Yeah. To Inverness. Where men are men and sheep are shagged." I put down the bag and we shook hands.

"Take care of yourself," he said. "I'll forward your mail."

"Thanks."

Jay came in. Stewart looked at me and went out. "I'm just going," I said to Jay.

She wore jeans and a jumper. She looked gorgeous. "Okay," she said.

"Cheer up," I said awkwardly. "You look like you need a good roll in the hay."

She gave me a vicious smile. "I'm just about to have one. Ian's waiting for me upstairs."

"Thanks." On my way out I knocked on Stewart's bedroom door. "Say goodbye to Debbie," I called.

"Yo."

I went.

Now it's winter. I haven't been back, but I'm sure she's still there. I wish I could have known her. These nights, I think of her sitting by the fire in the living room, with the cold around her. I miss her.

January, 1990

NORTHERN LIGHT

When somebody from Inverness dies and goes to hell, it seems like heaven. I stayed there for a few months, but it seemed like a long time. Then I left.

There was a bus going at two in the afternoon. I bought my ticket at one-fifteen. Behind me in the queue at the ticket office, a woman stood talking to herself. She had an American accent that didn't sound genuine. "Personally, I would not sleep with a bus driver," she said. "It's a matter of personal taste. Personally, I would not sleep with low-class people." I bought my ticket and left the office.

It was freezing. I didn't want to sit around the station till the bus came. I went to the Co-op to get something to eat and drink on the bus. All I had to carry was a big holdall. I hadn't brought much to Inverness, and I was leaving with little more.

In Church Street, a girl came up to me and said my name as a question. I looked at her and remembered long, dyed-black hair, goth clothes and lots of jewelry. Instead I saw brown hair in a tight perm, glasses with red plastic frames, a Pringle jumper and tweed skirt. Five years on, and she looked like the wife of a self-made man.

"Kathy," I said, still not sure it was her.

It was. She smiled at me. "I thought it was you. What're you doing in Inverness?"

I smiled back. I was pleased it was her. "Running away. I've been living here, but I'm clearing off today."

"I've been here for a week. We're in a flat in Tomnahurich Street," she said. She looked at me and laughed. "My God! I can hardly believe it's you."

"I'm surprised you recognized me."

"You haven't changed. Your dress sense is better though."

I didn't know about hers. "What're you doing here?" I asked.

"My husband's got a job here. On a fish farm." Seeing my look, she added, "I'm married now."

"How long for?" I said for something to say.

"Two years. What about you?"

"No."

"I wouldn't have thought Inverness'd be your sort of place."

"It's not," I said. "That's why I'm getting out of it."

"I like it."

I shook my head. "It's our national mentality. I mean, we're not the only country with a place like this. The Russians've got one. They call it Siberia, and use it as a penal colony. We call ours Inverness, and live in it."

She laughed and pushed me. "You haven't changed. Alasdair says a Glaswegian's a cross between an Englishman and a sheep."

I looked at my watch. One-forty. "Listen, my bus is at two. D'you want to go for a drink or something?"

"Yeah, but Alasdair's picking me up in the car. He'll be here at a quarter to two. I'll have to let him know."

"Ask him along."

"Yeah. He'll like you," she said. While we were waiting outside the Co-op, she asked me, "Are you still a journalist?"

"Not really. I was foreign editor of the *Dandy*, but they fired me for sending Desperate Dan to the Lebanon and getting him killed."

She smiled and shook her head. "Some things don't change."

Some things do. "My other stuff's doing quite well now," I said.

She nodded "I heard."

"Are you still nursing?" I asked.

"Only our baby. I haven't been working since I married. But I quit nursing anyway."

I hadn't expected the baby, but I hadn't expected anything. Her figure was all right. I was about to ask why she'd quit nursing, but at that point her husband arrived in his car.

He looked like you'd expect a Highland fish farmer to look. He'd a beard, wore jeans and a jumper, and there was a lot of him. There was a boy of about a year old in the car with him.

Kathy introduced us and we shook hands. He said she'd talked about me. "D'you fancy coming for a drink?" I asked him.

"Aye, fine." He gestured towards the kid. "But I'll have to take the menace round to my mother's first."

"I thought you were taking him earlier on," said Kathy.

"I was. But I'd to drive up to Brora. I'll take him now. Where'll I find you two?"

Kathy and I looked at each other. "Wherever you like," I told her.

"The Market bar?" she suggested. That's where we went.

It was an old, folky sort of pub, nearly empty at that time of day. I got Southern Comfort for her and Guinness for myself and we sat at a table.

"What's your kid's name?" I asked her.

"Alasdair. Same as his Dad."

"It's good to see you. Weird to see you up here."

"It's weird you being up here." She smiled. "Were you still in Glasgow before?"

"No. Edinburgh for a while. Some other places, too. What about you?"

"The Borders. That's where I met Alasdair. But his family's from Inverness, so we moved up."

"I'm surprised you quit nursing."

"That wasn't because I got married. I quit before."

"I know. You said. That's what I'm surprised at. I thought you were really into it."

"I was. But I couldn't do it. There was this boy of nineteen. He was in a car crash. When they brought him in, they had to drill through his skull, and they could only use local anaesthetic. They started before it was working. You should've heard him screaming. I was holding his hand, and he was nearly crushing it. I just kept telling him he was all right. I was crying myself, all the way through it. That's no good if you're a nurse."

"Fuck's sake."

"His parents were going to sue the hospital, and they wanted me to be their witness. I was going to do it. But I didn't have to. They dropped it. But that showed me I wasn't much use as a nurse. There doesn't have to be a mistake for some boy to scream."

"I know."

Alasdair arrived a few minutes later. He went to the bar, got a pint of heavy, and sat with us. We talked for a while. When I looked at Kathy I remembered, and when I looked at Alasdair I imagined him fucking her, or her sucking him off.

I left them at three-thirty. I shook hands with him and kissed her on the cheek (he was a pretty big guy) and they gave me their address and said if I was ever in Inverness again and so forth.

It was ridiculous. It'd been five years, but as I walked to the bus station I felt so betrayed. He seemed a nice enough guy, but I'd never have thought she'd be into that scene.

I got the bus at four. The mad American woman, if that's what she was, was still hanging around the station, talking to herself. I hoped she wouldn't get on my bus, but she did. Then she got back off it.

The bus took me out, across the bridge over the river. It was a sepia day. Overhead the gulls were wheeling, spinning.

January, 1990

TIDINGS OF COMFORT AND JOY

That Christmas I was back in Edinburgh. Princes Street on Christmas Eve was like it always is then, the dark of the early evening and the lights from the shops bouncing off each other. It was raining on and off. Because of the rain I spoke to Jay.

The rain had stopped and I'd taken off my glasses to wipe water from them, so I didn't see her coming. By the time I saw her she'd seen me too and it was too late to pretend I hadn't seen her and duck into a shop. And it hadn't got to where I could just walk past and ignore her.

She smiled uncertainly at me. She didn't have an umbrella and she was soaked. She wore jeans, boots, an overcoat and a strange little hat that must've come from Hippy Fashions, where she worked.

"Hi." I said.

She went on smiling. "Hi!" She seemed pleased to see me. "What're you doing in Edinburgh?"

"Nothing much."

"How long're you here for?"

"Just a couple of days," I lied. "Where're you headed?"

"The bus station. I'm going to my Mum and Dad's for Christmas. Where're you staying?"

I told her.

"So how are you?" she asked me.

"All right. How're things in the flat?"

"Some big changes since you left," she said.

"Like what?"

She hesitated. "A lot of things. Debbie and Paul for instance. Have you heard?"

"No. I'm not long back. Have they finished?" Debbie, who'd lived in the flat while I was there, had been having an affair with Paul, who worked with her and was married.

Jay smiled sourly. "They certainly have. You can't have been reading the *Sun*, or you'd know. About three weeks ago, Paul's wife was away for the weekend, so he came round to the flat for a session with Debbie. They went round to the Antiquary, and came back absolutely steaming. Especially Paul. He got up to go to the toilet in the middle of the night. He was so drunk he fell down the stairs and went right through the door at the bottom."

"Christ. Was he hurt?"

"He broke his neck. Debbie and I found him dead in the morning. Of course, I had to get the police in. So his wife found out what'd been happening, and we've hardly had the papers stop phoning us. Debbie had to give up her job and go back to Jersey."

Jay looked at me and realized I was grinning. "You really are sick, you know that?" she said. Then she started to laugh too, and she hugged me. "Sick bastard. Still the bloody same."

We talked for another few minutes, and she told me some other things. "D'you fancy going for a drink or something to eat?" I asked her.

She spread her arms. "I'd like to, but they're expecting me at home. I'm late as it is."

"Don't worry about it."

"Look, you'll be gone by the time I get back," she said. "But give me a ring next time you're in Edinburgh, okay?"

"Right," I said.

"I wish I'd more time," she said.

"So do I. Don't worry about it."

She kissed me very quickly. "Take care. Okay?"

I kissed her back. "You too."

I headed up towards the Old Town. It was raining again, but I didn't mind. It meant nobody could see I was crying.

February, 1990

THE MEDAL

for Sergio Casci

That winter, I worked for a social services magazine. It was the mouthpiece of a pressure group that was also a registered charity. That meant we were allowed to kick up enough shit to get noticed sometimes, but not enough to seriously annoy anybody.

The exception was the Old Les story. A social worker up in Roystonhill had tipped us off that this old guy had been discharged from Woodilea mental hospital under the "community care" scheme.

What "community care" means is that the hospital's so strapped for cash it has to kick people out and just forget about them. Most mental patients in Glasgow then end up in the Great Eastern Hotel, a kip for down-and-outs. Old Les was luckier, but not much.

Because of his age—seventy-one—the council found him a flat in Roystonhill. That's where we came in. Denise, our friend in the Social Work Department, phoned and told us we should have a look at the conditions Les was living in.

So we did. Every wall was foul with damp. Local kids had smashed all the windows. Les slept on a mattress on the floor. You could actually see the lice on it, though I was never sure whether Les had got them from the mattress or the other way round.

I'd come to see him with Serge, the magazine editor, and Andy, our photographer. I did an interview and Andy took some photos. We told Les we'd do what we could.

And we did. We phoned the council so many times that once the guy who answered said, "Christ. Not you again!" We ran a photo of Les on the front page of the magazine, and it stirred up so much interest that it appeared on breakfast TV—for all of thirty seconds.

Les got rehoused. The council moved him to Easterhouse, which some would say is a bit like being moved from Dachau to Auschwitz. But at least the flat had no damp, and the windows were too high to hit with stones.

We sent Andy along to get a photo of Les signing the papers for the flat. He printed up a couple of shots and showed them to Serge and me. Les was sitting in the council office, wearing an ancient suit and giving a pathetic thumbs-up sign.

Later that day, Serge came into my office holding one of the photos. "Did you notice he was wearing his medal?" he asked me.

I said I hadn't.

"Look. He is." Serge handed me the photo. He was right. There was a medal pinned to Les's coat. The coat looked as old as the medal.

"Yeah," I said, "I see it."

Serge laughed, strangely. "Poor old bastard!" Then he stopped laughing. "Poor old bastard."

September, 1989

QUEST FOR MAUREEN

At the third attempt, he found enough courage to dial the number and not hang up before it was answered.

A woman's voice said hello. It was the wrong woman's voice.

He said, "Hello. Can I speak to Maureen, please?" He should have been scared but he wasn't any more.

"Who do you want?" the woman said.

"Maureen," he said.

"I think you've got the wrong number."

"I'm looking for Maureen McConlogue. Is she there?"

"No."

"Do you know her?"

"No."

"Oh," he said. "Sorry."

"Were you at college with her?"

"What?"

"Were you at college with her?"

"That's right. I was."

"Are you going back next term?"

"So you do know her?"

"Yes. Are you starting back on Tuesday?"

"Is Maureen there?" he said.

"No."

"Do you know where she is?"

"She'll be starting back on Tuesday."

"Oh. She said she was." *So what? I won't be.*

"Are you going back?"

"Yeah," he said.

"You'll probably see her there on Tuesday, then."

"I probably will. Thanks."

"Bye."

"Bye," he said, but he was never sure if she'd hung up before he'd said it.

February, 1988

WHAT ABOUT THE MONSTER?

for Keith Mackie

"Christ's sake, Anne! It can wait till tomorrow!" Karen shouted at me, and I knew she was talking sense.

Only sense didn't make much sense at that moment. "I know. Or it could wait till next week. He's not going to die. But I'm still going now."

"You won't get a train at this time."

"I'll hitch," I told her. "There's plenty of lorry drivers."

"Great idea!" she almost screamed at me. "And what about the Monster?"

Karen followed me through to the bathroom in the flat we shared. I stood in front of the mirror and began fixing my make-up. It'd become smudged when I'd cried over the news about Sandy half-an-hour before.

"What about the Monster?" Karen repeated, sounding as though she might cry.

I didn't look at her or I might've changed my mind. "Don't worry. Of all the girls in Dundee, I doubt he's out there sharpening his knife specially for me."

"It's not impossible, though," she argued. "The other girls probably thought the same thing. It's stupid to go out asking for it. Please, Anne."

Five minutes later I left the flat, rucksack on my back. "You idiot!" Karen called as I went down the stairs. "He's not even your boyfriend any more!"

"That's why I'm going," I called back.

She was right, I thought as I walked along the deserted main road in the rain. Sandy wasn't my boyfriend any more. In fact, after he'd dumped me, I'd joked bitterly that, after a boyfriend like that, the Monster probably wouldn't be too bad. Karen, of course, looked shocked and told me not to be so sick.

Not that she was wrong, though. The Monster wasn't a person to joke about, especially if you happened to be one of his victims. The killings had started just after I'd moved to Dundee from Glasgow. He'd started with prostitutes, then seemed to decide that anyone would do, just as long as they were young and female. And he liked to keep busy; in the space of a year, he'd cut the hearts out of nineteen girls. And the police had no idea who he was.

The Monster's most recent victim was a girl I knew from college, so I really shouldn't joke about it. But my sense of humor's pretty sick. It was one of the reasons Sandy dumped me.

The rain got heavier and the road remained deserted. I didn't feel like joking when I thought about Sandy. Would he want to see me after losing his eye? I remembered the last conversation we'd had. Right out of the blue, as I was trying to undo his belt, he'd told me that it was over. Naturally, I asked him why.

"I've been trying to tell you for months." There then followed a veritable list of reasons for giving me the heave. Talk about opening the floodgates! He might've been unable to tell me for months, but he made up for it there and then. Once he'd explained how 1) stupid, 2) boring, 3) plain, 4) hopeless in bed I was, I'd long been in tears and Karen'd arrived at the flat. She kicked him out, but not before he'd added that, on top of everything else, I had the most warped sense of humour he'd ever come across. Upset though I was, I couldn't help calling after him. "You should've wiped it off, then!"

I saw the headlights of a car in the distance. I put my rucksack down and stuck out my thumb. The car stopped. A guy stuck his head out of the window. He was young, with a crew-cut. "Where you going?" he asked in an English accent.

I smiled at him. I've got a nice smile. "As far South as you're going. I'm trying to get to Glasgow, but I don't suppose you're going that far?"

He opened the door on the passenger side. "Get in," he said flatly. I realized he hadn't answered my question, but got in anyway. I closed the door and he drove off without looking at me.

He was probably about twenty. He'd the sort of face only a mother could love, and I doubt if even his mother was all that keen on his bovver boots and combat jacket. He looked like a cartoonist's impression of an NF thug.

Still, he gave me a lift. I sat in silence for about ten minutes. I didn't feel like talking, and I didn't know what to say to him anyway. *Mugged any old ladies lately?*

Instead, I just watched the headlights dart along the dark road in front of the car. And I thought about Sandy.

I'd been so pathetic when I'd started going out with him. I still cringe when I think of some of the things I used to say. He worked in insurance and was an aspiring yuppie. I was with him when he bought his first Filofax. That same evening, we sat on his sofa with the Filofax in my lap. "Sandy," I lisped, "know what I like about your Filofax?"

"What?" he asked, understandably baffled.

"I like the way the pages *turn*."

Yeuch.

The rain lashed the car window. "I'll be dropping you off soon," my chauffeur said. "What'll you do then?"

"Hope a lorry driver picks me up."

He looked at me, and I didn't like the look.

"Aren't you worried about the Monster?"

"A bit. Not very much," I said.

"You're a stupid bitch," he informed me.

"Sorry," I said, and silence reigned for another few minutes.

As far as I knew, Sandy and his Filofax were still together, though he and I were no longer one. And now, according to his mother when she'd phoned earlier that night, Sandy and his right eye had gone their separate ways. "He was attacked in the city center," his mum said. "The doctor says he'll be all right, but they had to take the eye out." A pause, then, "Will you come down, Anne? I know how he treated you, but it'd really help him to know you care"

And I did care, of course. Which is why I was out hitch-hiking on a night when every other woman in Dundee who wasn't actually retarded had her door locked. Sandy, I knew, wouldn't be able to understand that. He'd probably think I'd come to crow.

The car stopped suddenly. The guy sat and looked at me for a moment, and I felt my bowels twitch. Then, to my relief, he reached over and threw open the door on my side of the car. "Right. Out you get," he said.

I forced a smile. "Okay. Thanks for the lift." I picked my rucksack off the floor and slung it out of the car. I was getting out too when I knew, just knew, what was going to happen.

The guy was right, I agreed, as he seized me by the hair and dragged me into the car backwards. I was a stupid bitch.

"Are you okay?" a male voice asked. I'd have thought it pretty obvious that I wasn't. I was lying face-down in the middle of the road, and had been for at least an hour. It was the rain that revived me, or I'd probably have stayed unconscious all night.

My jeans, knickers and shoes were gone. Judging by the way my mouth felt, so were about half of my teeth. My head was covered in a mixture of blood and vomit.

"What happened?" the voice said. I raised my head from the puddle of vomit it lay in and looked at the speaker. He was fortyish and worried. There was a lorry parked nearby.

"I've been raped," I mumbled as he helped me to my feet.

There's not much you can say to something like that, and that's about what he said. I looked around me. There was no sign of my jeans, but my rucksack lay close by. The man picked it up. "Come on," he said as he helped me into his lorry. "You're going to need a doctor."

I sat back in my seat and closed my eyes. My body was shivering.

My rescuer got into the driver's seat. "I'm Martin, by the way," he told me.

"My name's Anne." My voice quavered. I opened my eyes.

Martin was looking awkwardly at my nakedness. "D'you want a towel or something to wrap round your waist?" he asked.

"There's a pair of jeans in my rucksack. And a jumper." I was trembling violently now. He handed me the rucksack and I opened it.

"Once we get you to hospital, we'd better call the police. Okay?" he said. I didn't answer. "D'you reckon it could've been the Monster who attacked you?" he asked.

"Not unless there's two of us," I said. I brought the knife out of my rucksack and slid it into his stomach. I let him scream for a while before I started to twist it.

As I said, I've got a pretty sick sense of humour.

November, 1987

THE PLACE

Eve got undressed right away, as soon as she'd found her room. It was only about ten and she wasn't tired, but that wasn't important. She wasn't sure what was any more.

The room was large, but somehow cell-like. There was no furniture except for two single beds, parallel to each other but on opposite sides of the room. Eve dropped her clothes on the green-carpeted floor, and got into one of the beds.

She wished she'd brought a nightshirt; she wasn't used to sleeping naked. The sheet felt slightly damp against her pale skin. It reminded her of something, though she wasn't sure what. She wasn't sure why she'd come here either. Something to do with Peter and a desire to lose control and also something about repressed sexual desires.

At least, that's what Barry had said. So it probably had something to do with him as well. She wasn't sure. But he'd promised to write, so maybe she'd know then.

Wasn't there also something about somebody loving her? Or just claiming to? Barry? Peter? She wasn't sure.

She wasn't comfortable. The bed was too short for her, but most of the beds she'd slept in were. She was exceptionally tall for a girl. Her dad said five-eleven, Barry said at least six feet. She believed her dad.

The electric light was harsh but she couldn't turn it off. There was no switch.

Eve closed her eyes and put a hand over them. She wondered what her room-mate would be like. She wondered why he'd come here. If he did. If anybody but her would really come. While she was wondering, he came into the room.

Hoping he'd think she was asleep, she looked at him through half-shut eyes. He didn't look at her. Even as she looked at him, she was forgetting what he looked like. Except that he was retarded and disgusting.

He took off his clothes and sat down on the other bed. Eve saw that there was a face on his right calf. It wasn't a tattoo. It looked like an actual face, a face on his leg.

It opened its eyes and smiled at her. She moaned in phobic horror and hid her face under the sheet.

Her room-mate tore the sheet away and came down on top of her. She felt his tongue in her mouth, the heat of his body against hers. He'd changed.

The following morning, Eve felt good. She went downstairs to reception and signed herself out. The man behind the desk laughed. Eve wasn't sure who he was laughing at.

She was standing in the rain, waiting for her bus, when she remembered why she'd come here.

March, 1988

WEDNESDAY NIGHT

three in the morning and so what? youre not around but that doesnt matter now does it? youre probably asleep with the darkness crouched outside your window like a pervert at the entrance to a childrens playground.

three in the morning three in the morning. old men finished lining up for soup in george square and wondering what to line up for now. god youre a bastard. papers talk about terrorists killing people in ireland and where else, do you have to look as far as ireland, cold kills people too or dont you know…

i dont know either but more than you. i love you and maybe/what if/i wish/i wish/IT HURTS IT HURTS…and…

three in the morning and not near you. old man got hit in the head with a hammer, now hes got a dent in his head so bad he gets a puddle when it rains. he unlocks door and opens it and sick yellow light spills out like pus escaping from a blister being burst. light or maybe just him has stale repellent smell like armpit of some geriatric prostitute.

three in the morning i walk around.

three in the morning i walk around.

face looking out from glass dark glass of shop window. face is gaunt. face is haunted. face is mine. water of leith three in the morning. heron wading across the water. heron will try to kill a fish. fish will die if it does and heron will die if it doesn't and so will you and i regardless…

i miss you miss you miss you miss you miss you

…………once upon a time.

………………three in the morning.

time goes slowly on the cold wet wooden bench youd be as well just sitting on the ground. stars in the sky when i was a child i used to think the universe was made of light and the sky was made of paper draped over the world to keep out the light like the cover on a birds cage. the paper had got worn and a few holes had appeared and the light was shining through and that was the stars. during the day god would take the cover off the world and we'd get all the light though we never really did get all the light.

men fishing at the water of leith i used to enjoy the company of fishermen now my sympathies are with the fish. the nearly affectionate way they talk about the creature theyre going to kill i wonder if theyd be hurt if they found out that the fish minded.

night and water and pin holes and fish. you. but not together and not making sense. to end with this. to end with this. to end with this.

August, 1987

THE KILLER

for Viv Grahame

I drank my tea amongst the hippies and housewives and schizo-phrenics and dossers in the afternoon heat. The Cornerstone Café is a dark place in the basement of a church in the shadow of Edinburgh Castle, but when it's warm they set up tables in the historical graveyard outside.

As well as being a haunt of blue-rinse Save-the-Whale types and people with beards, the Cornerstone's benevolence also makes it popular with down-and-outs and the mentally ill. Somewhere amongst all that, you used to be able to find me.

For most of one summer, I went there a couple of times a week. I never liked the place. But neither did any of my friends, and I wasn't feeling very sociable around that time.

I was sitting at a table in the graveyard. There were three others at the table, a man and two girls. I didn't know any of them. There was nobody sitting on the chair facing me.

Then the killer sat on it.

He was about forty, younger than most of the dossers you see there. He had brown hair that looked like he'd tried to cut it himself. His face was clean, but his hands were grey with dirt. His clothes looked like they were rotting. He'd a cup of some-thing, which the café'd have given him for free.

He grinned at me. I grinned back.

"I'm a killer," he told me.

"Are you?" I said. The others at the table were ignoring him, the man self-consciously eating his lentil bake and the two girls talking.

"Aye," he said. "I am." He looked at one of the girls. "Is that your girlfriend?" he asked me.

"No," I said. The girls worked hard at carrying on talking.

He gave one of them a prod. "Heh."

She stopped talking to her friend. "What?"

"Is he your boyfriend?"

"No," she told him with nervous coldness. She looked away.

"I told you she wasn't," I said.

He nodded. "I'll have to kill somebody soon," he said loudly.

"How come?"

"To prove I'm a killer."

"How come you have to prove it?"

"So people believe me."

I didn't say anything.

"People don't believe me."

"What if they don't care?" I said. He stood up and pissed in front of everybody. Then he left. People shook their heads and went back to eating or talking.

January, 1992

EITHER/OR

All I had to do was cut his face.

I was doing the *Evening Times* crossword when Duncy rang. Clare was watching TV. It was about eight in the evening.

When I realized it was Duncy, I took the phone through to the bedroom. He told me what he wanted and I asked if I could think about it and call him back.

He said I could.

I thought about it and called him back two minutes later. I asked if I could sub-let the job to somebody else and take a third of the money myself.

He said no.

He said he was only asking me because he knew me.

I said I'd phone and let him know. I hung up and went back through to the living room.

"That was Duncy," I told Clare.

"How's he doing?" Clare was forty, a year younger than me, and liked to know how everybody was doing.

"He wants me to do a turn," I said.

She laughed, then saw I wasn't joking. "Who for?"

"He didn't say. He's paying a thousand. It's a lot of money. It wouldn't go amiss."

She nodded, but didn't say anything.

"What d'you think?" I asked her.

"It is a lot of money," she said. She thought about it, then said, "It's up to you."

"We could be doing with a thousand," I said. We didn't actually need it, but it'd come in handy. The off-license we owned was only getting by, and our boy Stewart had just started at Glasgow University, which was costing us.

"It's up to you," Clare said again.

I took the dog for a walk, then phoned Duncy and said I'd

do it. He said I'd get five hundred up front and the other five after I'd done my turn. But I'd have to do it soon.

I said I'd do it the day after tomorrow.

Next day, I went to the fishing tackle shop.

I wasn't sure when to do it. I'd never heard of the guy, and Duncy wouldn't tell me anything other than that he lived alone and usually worked from home. Sometimes it's best to do it first thing in the morning, when they're likely to think it's the postman at the door. But that depends on who it is. If he knows the score and expects somebody to visit, early in the morning's when he'll be most wary.

Since I didn't know one way or the other, I decided around lunchtime was as good a time as any.

Clare kissed me and said good luck before I left the house. I felt a bit nervous, but not very. It was ten years since I'd done a turn and I couldn't remember if I used to feel like that.

The guy lived in Knightswood. I drove over there, along Great Western Road. I listened to Radio Snide, knowing that Clare would be listening to it as well.

It was blowing a gale.

The door to the foyer had an entry system. I thought of pressing the buzzer and saying it was the second post, but I was scared it might've already been. I waited to see if anybody'd go in or come out so I could grab the door, but nobody did. I pissed about with the lock, but I couldn't do anything with it.

So I kicked it in.

One kick did it, but it made a hell of a noise. I went into the foyer and closed the door after me. I stood and waited, hoping nobody'd come out of their flat to see what the crash was. Nobody did.

My customer lived on the second floor. I climbed the stairs and found the flat. I got out the lockknife I'd bought in the fishing tackle shop and opened it. Then I rang the doorbell.

When I heard him coming, I stepped to one side of the

door, just in case he was tooled up. But he'd no idea. He opened the door in his bare feet, wearing brown cord trousers and a jumper. He was about fifty, going bald, with a mustache. He'd a cigarette in his hand. I could hear the sound of Radio Snide coming from somewhere behind him.

I said his name, and when he said yes I drew the blade across his face. He just stood there and put his hand against his left cheek. A line of blood came from under the hand and ran down his neck.

"Oh, no. Oh," he said. I saw he still had the cigarette in his hand.

Then I remembered what I was meant to be doing. I cut his other cheek, but he moved and the blade cut through his lip as well. He started to whine and at the same time I thought I heard somebody else coming to the door, though I probably imagined it. I kicked him in the balls and he staggered back into the flat and I pulled the door shut and ran down the stairs.

"Did it go all right?" Clare asked me.

"Fine," I said. We were sitting in the kitchen. She'd just made some coffee. "I'll see Duncy tonight and get the rest of the money. It went fine."

"That's good," she said.

The next day, she left me and never came back. It was up to me, she'd said.

June, 1991

BARRY GRAHAM is a writer and performance artist and the author of several books of fiction. His past occupations have included grave-digging, drug-dealing, shoplifting, political activism and boxing. Born in Scotland, he now lives in Phoenix, Arizona. His most recent novel, *The Book of Man,* was chosen by the American Library Association as one of the Best of 1995. He is a serious student of Zen Buddhism and ethnopoetics.

incommunicado

INCOMMUNICADO PRESS ☆ SAN DIEGO

STEVE ABEE ☆ KING PLANET 146 pages, $12.

DAVE ALVIN ☆ ANY ROUGH TIMES ARE NOW BEHIND YOU 164 pages, $12.

ELISABETH A. BELILE ☆ POLISHING THE BAYONET 150 pages, $12.

IRIS BERRY ☆ TWO BLOCKS EAST OF VINE 108 pages, $11.

BETH BORRUS ☆ FAST DIVORCE BANKRUPTCY 142 pages, $12.

DAHLIA & RUDE ☆ ARMED TO THE TEETH WITH LIPSTICK 130 pages, $12.

PLEASANT GEHMAN ☆ PRINCESS OF HOLLYWOOD 152 pages, $12.

PLEASANT GEHMAN ☆ SEÑORITA SIN 110 pages, $11.

BARRY GRAHAM ☆ BEFORE 200 pages, $13.

R. COLE HEINOWITZ ☆ DAILY CHIMERA 124 pages, $12.

HELL ON WHEELS ☆ ED. BY GREG JACOBS 148 pages, $15.

JIMMY JAZZ ☆ THE SUB 108 pages, $11.

PETER PLATE ☆ ONE FOOT OFF THE GUTTER 200 pages, $13.

PETER PLATE ☆ SNITCH FACTORY 182 pages, $13.

SCREAM WHEN YOU BURN ☆ ED. BY ROB COHEN 240 pages, $14.

TENSE PRESENT ☆ ED. BY TOSCANO & VERDICCHIO 225 pages, $14

UNNATURAL DISASTERS ☆ ED. BY NICOLE PANTER 250 pages, $15.

SPOKEN WORD CDS: GYNOMITE! FEARLESS FEMINIST PORN, $14.
EXPLODED VIEWS: A SAN DIEGO SPOKEN WORD COMPILATION, $14.